The Many Lives of Veronica

Written by members of
Oklahoma City Christian Fiction Writers

Shannon D. Pearson, Editor.

The Professional Bridesmaid by Shannon D. Pearson
Unbeckoned by David L. Thornburg
Repairing Our Forever by Kristi Woods
The Letter in the Garden by Bill Garrison
Lock Down! This is Real by Katherine Webster
Black Wing Angel by Chris Tarpley

Published by
Oklahoma Christian Fiction Writers
Edmond, Oklahoma 73034 U.S.A.
Copyright 2021@Edmond, Oklahoma
by Shannon D. Pearson, David L. Thornburg, Kristi Woods, Bill Garrison, Katherine Webster, and Chris Tarpley.

Written by members of Oklahoma Christian Fiction Writers
     Editor - Shannon D. Pearson
     Cover Art by Samantha Fury

This book is dedicated to Darlene Franklin, founding member of Oklahoma Christian Fiction Writers and the genesis of our yearly story collections.

You were a mentor, a guide, and a great friend.

We miss you, Darlene, and can't wait to see you again.

The Professional Bridesmaid

By Shannon D. Pearson

The dress hung from a hook in her studio apartment. Veronica shuddered. Who picked lime green for their bridesmaids' dresses? Maybe as an accent color—a ribbon around the waist, a pair of shoes, or a fancy hairclip. But the entire dress? It would be like having five limes next to you on stage. At your wedding!

Maybe the lime dress had been chosen to spite her and the other bridesmaids. Veronica hadn't even met them yet, only met the bride and her parents. the groom and family would not be arriving until Friday night late. That pushed the rehearsal and ceremony into one long day. Bad luck for the couple to see each other on the wedding day, but Veronica had been overruled. Again.

"You need this paycheck," she reminded herself. She needed a new car, and maybe save some for college.

The bride's father had offered her triple the normal fee she usually received as a professional bridesmaid. And she had earned every penny. Michelle Johnson, the bride, had not wanted to make a decision. She'd even missed several appointments. She was the worst client. If Mr. Johnson wasn't with her, nothing got done. He'd chosen everything from tuxedoes to tablecloths, not to mention having decided on the venue, and caterers. Veronica felt like she was working for him, not the bride.

He was always talking about how this wedding would join two large companies, creating an empire. Veronica wasn't sure how marriage could join businesses—wouldn't that require a business merger? But that detail wasn't for her to worry about. The wedding ceremony and reception were her job.

She dressed in the outfit she'd wear to the rehearsal, black slacks and a custom bridesmaid shirt, complete with her name embroidered on the left shoulder. Everything about this wedding had to be custom to please Mr. Johnson. And he was willing to pay for it. It was time to get to the venue and make sure all the decorations were exactly right. She grabbed an espresso on her way out the door. She was going to need it.

Twelve hours until the reception was over, and she'd receive the second half of her payment.

She slipped into her little gray Honda and pulled onto the street. After half an hour, she pulled in front of the large church. Cars were already parked in the lot. She was supposed to arrive before everyone.

"Oh no." She hurried to put her things in the changing room. It was already a mess of lime dresses, and bags. "Please let this be the only mess I find." She'd spent yesterday decorating the sanctuary and reception hall.

She opened the doors to the sanctuary. Stained glass windows illuminated the stage, where four bridesmaids squabbled over decorations. Michelle watched from the floor.

Veronica closed her eyes a second, straightened her back, and marched forward. She clapped her hands. "Attention!"

The room quieted. Veronica looked at each girl, putting the names on their shirts with faces.

"Who's wedding is this?"

They glanced to Michelle, then back to her.

"Put everything back where you found it."

"Who do you think you are?" Blonde Felica had the perfect tan.

"She's the maid of honor," Michelle said.

Oh no, she didn't. Why not just paint a target on Veronica? Oh, wait she did. A lime target.

Veronica gave orders until everything was back in place. When it was, she turned to the bride. "How does it look?"

Michelle shrugged. "Not as good as when you did it."

Then why hadn't Michelle stopped them from messing with it? She clenched her teeth and pasted on a smile. "What do we need to fix?"

"It'll be fine."

"In what order would you like your maids to stand?" That was one thing Veronica never got Michelle to decide. Neither had she decided on a maid of honor until a moment ago.

"You choose." Michelle turned and walked out.

"The order you are sitting in then." She pointed at the painter's tape on the floor. "This is where you'll stand during the ceremony."

Her back would be to them. Thank heavens there would be hundreds of people watching, otherwise the women might stab her. "Shall we go to brunch?"

They stood and walked out, whispering.

Paycheck. Triple paycheck. Second half coming tonight. Just make it through today, and that new red Subaru was hers.

It was time to meet the men. Just like with the bridesmaids, she knew all their names but had never met a one. Not even the groom. It really had been the strangest wedding planning ever.

She surveyed the reception hall before entering. Mr. Johnson introduced her to the groom and his parents, then pointed out the groomsmen.

"Please find your nameplate," Mrs. Johnson said. "and have a seat. Food will be served shortly."

Veronica's seat was by the best man, Anton. He was good looking, like many of the groomsmen she met. He chatted loudly with his buddies about sports, and she listened, mostly letting conversations flow in one ear and out the other. This was always the awkward time. Friends and family conversations. She didn't know the people who were being talked about. It was time to be quiet and let them enjoy themselves.

She would enjoy the food. All sorts of fruits and cheeses lined the middle of the table. Servers brought juice and coffee. Then came an amazing quiche and coffee cake. When the meal was over, Mr. Johnson stood and started for the sanctuary. The others followed.

During the rehearsal, the back of Veronica's neck tickled.

One of the groomsmen snickered. What was going on?

She felt it again, something small, like a tap. Over the next few minutes, she felt it several more times.

Were the other bridesmaids throwing things at her?

"I present Mr. and Mrs. Dylan Davis," the priest announced.

The bride and groom walked out. Veronica met Anton centerstage and took his arm.

"Dylan tells me you're a professional bridesmaid." Anton glanced at her as they walked. "Think you can help me find a bride?"

"As if I haven't heard that line before." She pulled her arm back as they joined the bride and groom in the lobby.

They stood a few feet away from each other, silent, unlike usual lovebirds.

Oh, what was she saying? Every couple was different. Some were lovey-dovey. Some were simply happy to be in the same room.

Today, they would be married. Veronica's job would be done, and she'd be on the next one who were much easier clients, though there'd still be stress on the wedding day.

At the call of the priest, they all went back in for final instructions. Her area of the stage was littered with tiny white balls. Great, what did the bridesmaids do?

When everyone else went to get dressed, Veronica examined the stage. Spitballs. What was this, junior high? She picked them up, double checking for more.

She checked to make everything was ready. Fortunately, the staff had done their jobs well. Everything was as it should be.

On her way to the dressing room, she took a deep breath, steeling herself, and plastered on a smile. Voices echoed as she approached the door.

When she pushed it open, silence settled. Great, they'd been talking about her. And now she had to change clothes in front of them.

No.

Nowhere in her contract did it say she had to be in this dressing room. She grabbed her bag and dress and left, shutting the door on her way out.

"If she's your new bestie, why doesn't she want to hang out with you?" Felicia's voice came through the door.

"Maybe it's you she doesn't want to be around," Michelle snapped.

How many more hours until this nightmare was over? Six. She prayed for no more difficulties.

Would a professional groomsman have this much trouble? Doubtful. Did they even exist? Maybe.

Veronica got ready in the ladies' bathroom, dressing, freshening her makeup, and fixing her hair. She looked dreadful, but who wouldn't wearing lime green?

She went back to the sanctuary, finding the photographer already setting up. She asked him, "Do you need anything?"

"Are the groomsmen ready?"

"I'll go check and direct them this way."

A few moments later, she knocked on the men's changing room.

"Is it the pizza?" Anton opened the door, tuxedo clad. His smiled dropped. "May I help you?"

"The photographer is ready for you all." She glanced past him to the other tuxedoed men.

"Put on your pretty smiles, boys." Anton called behind him.

"Did you really order pizza?"

"A man's gotta eat."

"I'll see what I can find to protect the tuxes." Pizza grease was the last thing they needed. She started down the hallway.

"You don't have any faith in us?"

She glanced back over her shoulder seeing them heading to the sanctuary. "Accidents happen."

In the kitchen, she looked for man-sized bibs. What was as big as a man? She saw a box of trash bags and pulled it out. They were large enough to cover a whole torso.

She brought a bottle of water for each for the groomsmen, along with a pile of napkins and the trash bags. She was headed to give the photographer a bottle of water when she saw the pizza guy.

"This way." She led him back. After getting their buffet set up, she cut holes in the trash bags.

Men's voices echoed down the hallway. They were returning.

She met Anton at the door. "Your pizza is here. And this is your bib." She held out a trash bag.

"Bib? No way I'm not..." He burst into laughter. "A trash bag? Are you kidding?"

"It'll get the job done." She lifted it waiting for him to insert his head. Then she helped him get his arms through. "Anyone else planning to eat pizza?"

A few raised their hands, she helped them into bibs. "Enjoy and be careful."

When they were settled, she returned to the women's dressing room. She knocked and pushed open the door. "Everybody ready? It's time for pictures."

Michelle still sat in her rehearsal outfit. The others at least had their lime on.

"What's going on?" Veronica tried to stay calm.

"I don't like that dress." Michelle said.

"But you..." Had she picked out the dress, or had her father?

"Knock, knock." Mrs. Johnson entered the room. "Michelle, why aren't you dressed? The photographer is waiting. Come, let's get a move on."

Together, Veronica and Mrs. Johnson dressed Michelle, a life-size doll who only cooperated at her mother's prodding.

"Out the door, ladies," Mrs. Johnson commanded.

They obeyed, following her to the stage. The photographer told them where to stand or sit, and pictures began.

***

Four bridesmaids went through the doors to the sanctuary, and then it was Veronica's turn. She stepped through, going slowly for the photographer, walked down the aisle with her stage-smile in place, and stopped at her place on the stage. The music reached its crescendo, and Michelle entered, radiant and eyes wandering the guests. Most brides only had eyes for their groom. Gracefully, she sailed down the aisle on her father's arm. They paused below the stage, and the priest welcomed everyone, and asked them to sit.

Veronica's mind wandered. The ring! Michelle had never given her the groom's ring. She couldn't sneak off and get it, even if she knew where it was. What an embarrassment. Would Mr. Johnson dock her pay? What could she do? Nothing. Just wait for disaster and hope Michelle had given the ring to Felicia.

"Is there reason these two should not be joined in Holy Matrimony?"

"Yes!" A handsome twenty something man in a baby blue shirt ran up the aisle. "Michelle is my wife."

Gasps flittered across the room.

Veronica wanted to laugh. This was a joke, right? She'd spent months helping Michelle plan. No, forcing her to plan.

Dylan stepped aside as the man joined Michelle and took her hand.

"What's the meaning of this?" Mr. Johnson stood.

"Daddy, you wouldn't listen. I love Jacob. We eloped last week. I can't marry Dylan. We're barely friends. We can't join your empires together."

Mr. Johnson face was red. Veronica hoped he wouldn't explode.

"Besides," Dylan said. "I've had a thing going with the maid of honor for some time."

"Excuse me?" Veronica could not believe her ears. She'd just met the man that day.

He peered around Michelle. "No, not you. Felicia." He held out his hand.

The woman left her place behind Veronica and went to stand beside him. Two couples. Bride already married, but not to the groom.

Veronica looked at Mr. Johnson. What would he do? Accept his daughter's marriage? Disinherit her?

Mrs. Johnson stood, joining Mr. Johnson. The Davises stood, and the four parents came onto the stage.

Veronica stood still and listened to the whispered conversation.

"What were you thinking, eloping?" Mr. Johnson said. "We've been planning this wedding for months."

"*You've* been planning," Michelle said. "And not listening. So, I gave up. You wanted this event, an elaborate wedding with all your friends watching. We walked down the aisle. But I'm not marrying Dylan. Jacob is my love."

"Honey." Mrs. Johnson took her hand. "You should have told us."

"I did. Dad took my car away and hired a professional bridesmaid to make sure the wedding happened."

No wonder Michelle had been so hard to work with. This wasn't *her* wedding.

Mr. Johnson turned to Veronica. "Did you know about this?"

"No." She hoped she still looked as shocked as she felt.

"What do you propose we do now?" Mr. Johnson asked.

Why was he asking her? "Well..." She tried to formulate the logistics. "We can proceed with a different groom."

"And become a laughingstock?"

Veronica felt the eyes of the crowd. "They aren't laughing. Even if they were, they aren't involved in this. Neither am I. This is between you and your daughter."

Was she fired now? At least she'd gotten half of her pay up front. That didn't cover all her stress, but if she had to cut her losses, it would do.

"He's blue collar." Mr. Johnson turned back to Michelle. "He can't provide for your happiness."

"Money doesn't guarantee happiness. I don't need the big house, pool, and staff. I just need a man who loves me and treats me right."

Money. How much money had Mr. Johnson spent on this wedding? Veronica knew. She'd been in charge of the budget. Money could not replace love. Veronica held her breath. What would Mr. Johnson decide? Daughter or reputation? Family or pride?

Mrs. Johnson nudged him, and he held out his hand to Jacob.

"Let's do this thing right." Mr. Johnson said. They shook hands. He turned to Mr. Davis. "I'm sorry."

"Us too. A nice dream, but our kids have different ones."

"Felicia, will you be my maid of honor?" Michelle held out her hand to her.

"Of course."

Veronica took two steps back so Felicia could take her place. Finally, a decision from the bride.

"Here." Dylan took off his suit coat and gave it to Jacob.

"Will you be my best man?"

"Sure."

The men shifted down. Jacob pulled two rings from his pocket giving one to Dylan and the other to Felicia.

"Let's start over." Mr. Johnson led the rest of the parents away from the altar.

Aside from the fact that the priest had to ask Jacob his name, the rest of the ceremony went smoothly.

Only a few minutes had passed when he said, "I present to you Mr. and Mrs. Jacob Fisher."

The happy couple walked out, followed by Dylan and Felicia. Then, Anton escorted Veronica out. It was over. Now just a couple hours of festivities, which would run themselves.

"So, Veronica," Felicia said. "Could you help with my wedding?"

She pasted on a smile. "We'll talk about that later." She was not committing one way or the other.

"Don't forget helping me find a bride," Anton added.

Was he still on that? Was he flirting?

"There's been enough drama for one day," she said. "Let's just hang out and enjoy the reception."

"You're on." He escorted her to the half full reception hall. Some guests must have left.

"Let's see what they have to eat." Anton steered her toward the food tables.

Veronica laughed. "Is food all you think about?"

"When my stomach is empty."

They filled some plates and stood against a wall making small talk. She learned basic things about him. He was a linebacker at his college, which explained his constant hunger.

The DJ announced the bride and groom. They did all the traditional things, then started mingling with the crowd. Another step closer to the day being over.

"I'd like to apologize." Michelle stood beside Veronica. "I gave you a lot of grief when really it was my father I was mad at."

"I understand that now." She put on a smile, not sure she wanted to be friends with Michelle but ready for the angst between them to be gone.

Michelle hugged her, then went on to the next conversation.

Veronica let out a breath of relief. Done. And everything had resolved.

When Michelle tossed her bouquet, Felicia caught it.

"I gotta split." Anton wiped his face with his napkin.

When he left, Veronica moved to the kitchen where she found Mr. Johnson handing an envelope to the catering manager.

"Oh, good." He handed her one with her name on it. "I don't have to track you down."

She smiled. "Thank you." It was over.

***

Author's note: I wrote this story with a lime pen. Yes, I write with pen and paper. It can be taken anywhere, and toddlers will try to push buttons on a computer or put their heads right between me and the screen.

Unbeckoned

By David L. Thornburg

Oklahoma City Memorial Hospital

"Gardner? Gardner!"

Veronica blinked in the harsh fluorescent lighting of the hospital. Her mind had drifted as she waited for the head of security to give her an assignment, but now she focused on a round, pink face squinting at her.

She was wearing a similar uniform to his, minus the badges and patches. She arrived at her temp security job for the day in an apathetic fog, with little conscious thought or effort on her part. Same song, second verse. Or hundredth verse.

His name tag said Sgt. Glenn Kersey. "Are you with me? Ready for duty?"

"Yes, sir. Sorry, sir." Deference seemed to be the best strategy.

"Your post is outside Room 703," he said. "The usual. A mental case picked up on the street. Had a run-in with the police. Make sure he doesn't harm himself or anyone else until the county can pick him up tomorrow. I don't think even you could mess this up. Don't leave until your relief arrives."

"Got it."

"And Gardner?"

"Yes?"

"No overtime."

She nodded, thinking it best not to ask how she could avoid it if her relief didn't show. She worried that Sgt. Kersey might not be able to hold two opposing thoughts in his mind.

She walked down the hall, orienting herself to the unfamiliar surroundings. This was her first-time working security in a hospital. Busy nurses in scrubs and colorful sneakers fluttered past her carrying clipboards, electronic tablets, medicine, and supplies.

Suspended from the roof was a metal sign with arrows showing the way to Admitting, Emergency, Cafeteria, and Elevators.

She followed an orderly pushing an empty wheelchair onto the elevator. He pushed three and looked at her quizzically.

"Seven, please."

It stopped on every floor, of course. Good thing she wasn't in a hurry.

She exited the elevator. To the right down the hall was a man in a uniform like hers, leaning back in a chair, the wall the only thing holding him up. Good thing it was a sturdy wall, because the man's bulk draped over the sides of the seat. He looked up from his phone as she approached.

He looked at her name tag. "Gardner? Nice of you to show." The guard wobbled to a standing position. He cocked his head toward the open door of Room 703.

She looked past him to the figure lying in the bed, covered to his chin with a thin sheet. His hair was unkempt, and his beard was scraggly and several days old. Maybe mid-thirties—hard to tell when they were unconscious. One arm was at the side of the bed, handcuffed to the rail. She looked at the dry erase board and saw the patient's name listed as John Doe.

The other guard handed her a key to the handcuffs.

"What's the story?" she asked.

"I was here when they brought him in. He was in a filthy leather jacket and torn jeans. Not stylishly torn, either. More like ripped to pieces. He was hollering about not knowing where he was and how they had to let him go. He got free of the two cops who were holding onto him. I don't think they thought he had the strength. He ran, bouncing off the walls like a pinball, bumping into people and turning over supply carts. I was talking to a cutie over at the nurse's desk, so I helped them get him under control."

"Typical tweaker," Veronica said.

"Funny, though, the nurse said the tox screen came back negative for everything except the sedative they injected him with."

This might be an easy gig after all, Veronica thought.

"Why the security, then?" she asked. "Seems like a holding cell at the city jail would be less expensive. Especially if he's not physically injured."

"That's above my pay grade," the guard said. "In fact, I stopped caring"—he looked at his watch— "I'm clocking out."

"No overtime," she said to his retreating back.

Without turning, he said, "You'll go far in this organization, Gardner."

She looked inside the room. The patient wasn't as unconscious as she first thought. He moaned softly and shifted, his eyelids fluttering.

His lips were moving. She stepped into the room and leaned over him to make out what he was saying.

"I want to stay," she heard him mutter. "Please. Let me stay."

It must be the sedative speaking. His eyes were wide open and staring at her. He reached for her, but the handcuff stopped him short.

"Help me," he said. "Help me stay."

She backed away. A doctor entered the room. Brushing past her, he said to the man in the bed, "Awake, are we? That wasn't supposed to happen for quite a while." As he logged into the laptop on a stand beside the bed, he looked at Veronica. "New here?"

She looked from the man in the bed to the doctor. He was African American, slight and medium height with close-cropped salt-and-pepper hair. His scrubs had tiny guitars on them.

"Is it that obvious?"

"Not at all. I just haven't seen you before, and the newbies usually get the graveyard shift." He read the screen, occasionally tapping the keyboard. He looked at the patient. "They gave you a pretty powerful knock-out dose, so I can't give you anymore. It would be better if you tried to rest." The doctor turned to Veronica. "Are we closer to learning his name? I hate to see 'John Doe' on a chart."

The patient got agitated. "Not Doe. Name is…" His voice trailed off as his face clouded in confusion, and Veronica felt pity for the poor man.

"There, there," the doctor said, pulling the sheet back up around the shoulders. "I'll be back later. We can talk then." He entered some more info on the computer, then crossed to the dry erase board, where he wrote *Strickland* beside the word doctor.

"The nurses will check in on him. Have the desk page me if there's any change."

"I will, Dr. Strickland."

"Call me Dwain."

"I'm Veronica."

He smiled. "If he gets upset, let me know. The dose they injected him with should stun an elephant."

"Why is he here instead of the jail?"

"The doctor on duty when he was admitted briefed me. A couple of cops were making a bust after following up on a tip about a drug exchange. They had everyone controlled when this guy seemed to appear out of nowhere, right behind them. He jumped on one of them. Lucky they didn't shoot him. He seemed disoriented, so they brought him here, thinking he was on something."

"Only he wasn't."

"Right. The bull-in-a-china-shop performance after he got here earned him the handcuffs."

"What's next?"

"Probably arraignment, followed by a psych eval. But we'll take care of him tonight."

"Yes, sir. Uh, Dwain."

"Great. We'll probably see each other a lot, at least until you get some seniority and leave us midnight rats behind." He grinned as he left.

Veronica considered sitting outside the room, then thought better of it. There was no threat out there. And sitting inside the room might give the patient a little comfort. She positioned an orange faux-leather chair where she could watch the bed and sat.

The patient lay still, staring at the ceiling. An hour passed, the subdued activity of a hospital floor in the dead of night passing outside the open door.

Veronica fought the urge to scroll on her phone or, worse, close her eyes. She watched the display on the monitor over the head of the bed—pulse, temperature, and respiration, punctuated by the hum of the blood pressure cuff tightening and the hiss of it releasing.

She slid her attention to the patient and found he was staring at her.

"Do you need anything?" she asked.

"Monroe. My name is Monroe." He inclined his head to the dry erase board.

"Do you want me to write it on the board?"

His nod was barely perceptible.

A marker was suspended on a string. She removed the cap. "Is that your first name or last?"

"Just Monroe."

She wrote it in parentheses next to John Doe.

"Tired," Monroe said.

"That's the medicine."

"No. Tired of moving."

He wasn't moving much. "What do you mean?"

"Moving in time. I just want to stay."

"Sorry," Veronica said. "I don't know what you mean."

"So many places... times. Why would God do this to me?"

Veronica glanced over her shoulder, hoping some help might arrive from the hall. Maybe this would be a good time to page Dwain.

"How can I help you?" she asked.

Monroe turned away from her and stared at the opposite wall.

Since he was quiet, she sat again. She wondered what God had to do with this. Monroe had said the words with bitterness, yet in Veronica's experience, God didn't interact in real life all that much.

She hadn't thought about God for a long time. Her college courses and part-time security work grounded her in the real world, where obvious causes determined absolute effects. If she were honest, she preferred a pragmatic view of things. Much more comfortable than worrying about what some distant God expected from her. One knew where one stood.

Even if the effects of such a practical view could be harsh. Like her favorite aunt dying when she was in junior high, though her church prayed for her healing. You couldn't predict the outcome of prayer, apparently, but rest assured that Stage 4 liver cancer led to the result you expected.

Her aunt's illness and death almost caused her to decline the gig in the hospital tonight. Memories bombarded her of her aunt's last stay. The unfortunate souls confined to their beds, their relatives looking drawn and tired, if they were lucky enough to have relatives with them at all.

She definitely preferred bank lobby security duty. Or department stores. Or sporting events. Anything but hospitals.

But money was money, and she needed some. She was a little older than most of her fellow students and couldn't bring herself to live in the dorms or student housing, and regular residential apartments were expensive. The hospital shift was better than nothing.

She hated reporting to a new place, though. New co-workers, new environment, and new supervisors. Maybe when she got her degree, she could get some stability in her life.

"I'm feeling clearer, now," Monroe said, turning over on his side, resting his cheek on his cuffed wrist. "That shot was like getting a cloud injected into my brain. Who are you?"

"My name is Veronica. I'm here to keep an eye on you."

Monroe gave a tight smile. "What a polite way to describe being my jailer."

"Do you remember how you got here?"

He squinted in concentration. "I was working in an English language school in Namibia. The principal there was ready to resign, give up and go home, though the students needed her very much. I was trying to take some of the burden off her shoulders. She even took a vacation, she trusted me so much. When she returned, she had her spark back. You could see it in her eyes."

"I meant, do you remember earlier tonight?"

"I was getting to that. About one thirty in the morning in Windhoek, I had the feeling in my stomach I always get."

"Windy Hook?"

"The capital city of Namibia," he replied, as if he couldn't believe the gaps in her education.

"Did it wake you?" she asked, deciding to go along with him. She had nothing better to do.

He shook his head. "I don't sleep much. It was the burning I get before I go to a new place. I flashed to that alley where the police were arresting those guys. I was too late to make a difference there."

She tried not to let the doubt show on her face, but she must have scowled.

"You don't believe me, do you?" His head dropped back onto his pillow. "That's OK. You asked."

It surprised Veronica to find she felt bad for not believing his ridiculous story. He couldn't help his break with reality. The least she could do was humor him. Perhaps talking would keep him calm.

"How many times have you jumped from one place to another?" she asked.

"Hundreds." His voice was weaker again.

"Why?"

"There's always something for me to do."

"How do you know what it is?"

"God tells me. You believe in God, don't you?"

She wanted to give him an honest answer, even if he was crazy. "I suppose so," she said, "but He's never said anything directly to me."

"Sure, he has." Monroe rubbed his cuffed wrist.

Veronica went to the sink and held a washcloth under cool water from the faucet. She draped it over his shackled wrist.

"That feels good," Monroe said. "Soothing. I don't experience a lot of kindness."

"So, are you like that TV show where the angel drops in on people's lives, fixes everything, then moves on?"

"I'm no angel," he said with a snort. "Besides, on that show the angel liked her work. I just want it to stop."

"I heard you say you wanted to stay. What did you mean by that?"

"I'm tired of it. I just want to stay in one place, see the same people, maybe take a little instead of giving all the time. I'm just a normal man, after all."

"Normal people don't bounce around from place to place. Normal people don't hear God talking to them. How did it start?"

When he closed his eyes and said nothing, she thought he'd gone to sleep, which was probably for the best. After several minutes, she considered turning on the TV, if only to keep herself awake.

Dwain's entrance rescued her from drowsiness.

He held a cup of coffee. "I didn't know how you took it," he said, handing it to her.

"The most important thing is hot," she said. "Thanks."

"Don't mention it." He scanned the monitor. "Anything to report?"

"He's been talking, but not making much sense."

Dwain nodded. "Maybe he'll say something that will help us help him. I'm afraid that if he gets absorbed in the system, he might not get the assistance he needs. Do you want anything else?"

She lifted her cup like she was making a toast. "No thanks, I'm good."

After he left, she blew across the top of the steaming liquid and sipped. When it was gone, she stood, stretched, and walked around the room. She pulled her phone out—2:37.

"College." The whisper came from the bed.

"What?"

"You asked me how it started. Something bad happened in college. A fire in the men's dorm. I was at a Bible college in Texas. Everybody died but me. Six other guys. I knew them all. Why did I get out? What made me special? What was God's will? Do you ever wonder about things like that?"

She didn't but thought maybe she should. She stayed silent.

"After that I came unfastened from time. I don't know how else to describe it."

Veronica should call Dwain, but she wanted to hear more. If the doctor came back in, she feared Monroe would stop talking.

"What happened wasn't your fault, was it?"

"*Vis major.* College Latin for 'an act of God.'" Monroe coughed and shivered under the sheet. He held his stomach and moaned.

"What's wrong?"

"It's happening. I feel it."

Veronica didn't know what to expect, but it relieved her when he didn't disappear.

"It passed," he whispered. "Sometimes it does. Can I go to the bathroom?"

She considered buzzing for a nurse, but she didn't need any help. What would they think if she bothered them over this?

She fished for the key in her shirt pocket and unlocked the cuff from around the rail. He sat up, and Veronica helped him off the bed. She guided him and the monitor stand into the restroom.

"Sit down."

He did. She hooked the handcuff to the handicap bar on the wall.

"So little trust," he murmured.

"I'll give you some privacy." She closed the door but didn't latch it.

Veronica paced the room at loose ends. She didn't want to crowd Monroe, but she felt she should be available if he needed something. The muted sounds of the monitor seeped through the door.

Several minutes went by. She was considering knocking on the door when she heard the monitor's noises slide into a single unbroken beep. Was he dead? She should have called for the nurses, after all.

She opened the door. The monitor's cords dangled, unattached. The toilet was unoccupied, and the handcuffs hung from the handicap bar, the end that had circled his wrist still closed. She peered in the shower, but he wasn't there.

She dashed out of the bathroom and into the hall, frantically looking both directions. No Monroe, but she saw Dwain talking with a nurse several yards away.

She ran to him. "He's gone!"

"What do you mean?" he asked.

"He vanished."

He followed her as she ran back to the room. "I let him go to the bathroom…"

Dwain scanned the room, then went into the restroom.

"Where could he go?" His eyes darted to every corner.

She knew it would seem crazy, but she told him about Monroe's claims.

To her relief, he didn't comment on how absurd it sounded. "Call the rest of security. I'll keep looking."

She should have done that from the start. She pulled the walkie-talkie from her belt and put the rest of the night team on alert. "He was in a gown and nothing else, so he shouldn't get far," she finished.

"You know you've got to call the sergeant," one voice reminded her.

The lump that rose in her throat almost stopped her breathing. "Copy that."

Her fingers shook as she pulled the contact info card from her pocket and dialed the boss's cell phone.

"Yeah?" answered a sleepy, gruff voice.

"Sgt. Kersey? This is Veronica Gardner at the hospital."

"Who? Oh, yeah, the temp. Did one of the guys put you up to calling me? I get very cranky at pranks."

"I'm afraid there's a situation," Veronica said, her oxygen only arriving in shallow gasps. "Our John Doe has escaped."

The voice lost its sleepiness. "You're kidding me! You had one job."

"I can't explain it, sir. I followed procedures."

"I'm sure you did." The sarcasm was so thick that Veronica could almost feel it coming through the phone. "I've got some calls to make. I'll get you some help to find him. You have thirty minutes to call me back with good news.

Otherwise, I'll come down there myself. You do not want me to come down there."

"Yes, sir. I mean, no, sir."

"Enjoy your last half hour on the job. Make it count."

Kersey hung up.

The ding of the elevator door caught Veronica's attention. The door slid open, and three guards exited. She approached them. "John Doe answers to the name of Monroe," she said. "White male, mid to late thirties, dark hair, several days growth of beard, about 170 pounds. In a hospital gown and barefoot."

A nurse at the desk said, "This might help." She set a laptop on the counter, facing the guards. On the monitor was the photo taken of Monroe when he was checked in.

The tallest guard's name tag said Reiser. He turned to the others. "Go back to your floors and do a room by room. Don't forget supply closets. Stay on channel three, and check in when you're finished." The other two headed back to the elevator. "Take the stairs," Reiser said. "We know he's not in the elevator."

He watched them enter the stairwell, shaking his head. He pulled his walkie-talkie and depressed the button on the side. "London, are you awake?"

A woman's voice answered. "Of course."

"Are you checking the video feeds?"

"I haven't seen the patient on any camera. I'll let you know if I do."

"Thanks." Reiser clipped his walkie and looked at Veronica. "Scour every inch of this floor. I'm going back to six to check it out." He looked at her name tag. "Gardner. You owe us big time for ruining our peaceful evening."

He hurried to the stairs without waiting for a response.

Dr. Dwain approached her, looking at her with pity. "Do you have any ideas?" she asked.

He shook his head. "I'll keep watch, but I need to make my rounds."

Veronica started checking the rooms. In the first, the patient was sleeping, thankfully, and didn't stir when she turned the light on in the bathroom to look. The next door was a supply closet, also empty. She searched methodically, seeing one sick person after another, each reminding her in some way of her aunt. The lady in 710 was unnaturally thin, like her aunt at the end. A woman in 706 was holding vigil beside her husband's bed, napping fitfully, like her mother, who'd stayed at the hospital for weeks nursing her aunt.

When she got to 707, the older man shifting restlessly in discomfort brought back memories she never wanted to have again.

She considered leaving the hospital, simply abandoning ship. How much worse could it be for her? She was certain to be fired anyway. At least it would be over faster.

Her stubbornness wouldn't let her do it. Besides, where would she live when the rent came due at the first of the month and she was unemployed?

She entered 705. The room was empty, but the bed was unmade. Maybe this patient transported out of there like Monroe did. That would be nice right about now. Just warp away from this entire night. She opened the bathroom door.

What was Monroe's deal, anyway? She imagined him waking up in a different part of the world, getting his bearings and waiting for God to tell him what to do. Tell him how he could help. Make the world a better place.

Maybe he *was* an angel.

She was surprised to find it comforted her to think that God would care enough about some people to send help. Maybe she could be used like that, some day. Or maybe He could send *her* some help today. "God help me," she said under her breath and immediately felt like a fraud for asking. She hadn't talked to Him in quite a while.

The bathroom was empty. She turned the light out, then paused. Something about the ceiling caught her eye. She turned the light back on and looked up. One tile was cracked in the center, as if it was collapsing under its own weight.

Or as if someone had stepped on it.

She dashed to 703 and opened the bathroom door.

She looked at the dangling handcuffs closely. One end was fastened to the handicap bar, but the other end only *looked* fastened. She opened it without using the key. Monroe's wrist hadn't evaporated into thin air after all. He must have picked the lock.

She looked up. All the ceiling tiles were in place, but what if...?

Veronica climbed onto the sink and stood, balancing precariously. One push on the tile directly above her and it lifted easily. She slid it to the side and pushed her head up through the hole.

It was dark except for the tiny shaft of light from the cracked tile in 705. She tried to let her eyes adjust, but before they did, she heard a scuffling noise. She saw a slight movement in the distance. Or was it her imagination?

Then a beam of light appeared several yards away. Someone had taken another tile out, and the room below shot its light into the crawlspace. A silhouette was bent over the opening. It looked in her direction. It was Monroe.

She hopped off the sink and darted into the hallway, then raced in the light's direction. She got passed three rooms, then stopped in the center of the corridor.

Dr. Dwain looked up from his work in a room with an open door. She put a finger to her lips so she could hear which way Monroe moved.

There was a sudden crash from the room to her right. She yanked the door open to a small chapel, where a pile of broken acoustic tiles littered the floor, a trail of dust led to two bare legs, poking down from the ceiling.

Dwain was at her side, and together they each grabbed a leg and lowered Monroe to the floor.

Despite his squirming, Veronica got her set of zip ties on his wrists. "Bet you don't get 'unfastened in time' from these, Monroe," she said.

"Please let me go," he pleaded. "I've got to go where I'm needed."

"Trust me, there's no one you can help more than me, if you'll just stay put until the police come for you."

She called on Channel 3 for some help, and the other guards appeared shortly and helped get Monroe secured back in 703. Dwain administered another sedative, and Monroe was soon sleeping soundly.

Reiser said, "Call the boss. He'll be relieved not to have to come back to work in the middle of the night. I'll leave Jenkins here with you for backup."

"I appreciate it."

Before he left, Reiser said, "You'll never hear this from Sgt. Kersey, but at least you recovered him. No telling how far he'd have gotten if you hadn't tracked him down."

With Jenkins at Monroe's side, Veronica called the sergeant and told him everything was under control. Reiser was right, Kersey didn't have any kind words. "Gardner, you're safe until your next hare-brained mess up." He hung up.

At seven, with the morning sun sliding through the window blinds, a police officer entered the room, Dwain behind them.

The officer was a short woman, not much older than Veronica. Her black hair was pulled back in a severe bun that peeked out under the back of her cap. Her name tag identified her as Dixon.

"It's Sam, all right."

"Sam?" Veronica asked.

"Sam Monroe. Slippery Sam. A regular Houdini, this one."

"The cops last night didn't know his name."

"One guy we arrested last night filled us in. He's Sam's brother, and he worried about him. If he misses his medication, he can be a real handful. Was he any trouble?"

Veronica caught Dwain's eye. "Nope. No trouble. So, he lives around here?"

"Born and raised. He's always been a petty criminal, though he's smarter than the average crook. But that's not saying much. He's so quiet that he seems to show up out of nowhere, and he's quite an escape artist. It's almost a miracle you kept him here."

A miracle. It didn't seem like a miracle. Not compared to what she was almost persuaded to believe a few hours ago. Instead, she was still in the middle of her grimy world, where nothing existed that she couldn't see, nothing that she couldn't touch.

She looked at the frail, powerless man in the bed. What a fool she was. Her lot was to do the best she could, struggle to get what she needed, and keep her head down. Anything else invited disappointment.

"All right," Dixon said, "Let's get him into a wheelchair." She shook Monroe roughly. "Wake up, sleeping beauty."

A nurse entered the room with a chair.

Veronica cut the zip ties, and they lifted him to a sitting position.

Monroe's eyelids fluttered. "I want to stay. Leave me alone..."

"I have to take you downtown. Your brother's waiting for you."

"I don't have a brother." Monroe moaned as they slid him to the edge of the bed and lowered him into the wheelchair. The prisoner mumbled incoherently as Dixon cuffed his left wrist to the armrest.

Veronica felt sorry for him. But not as sorry as she felt for herself. How could she have believed this sick, pathetic man even for a second?

The nurse spun the chair toward the hall and pushed.

"Wait!" Monroe said loudly. He grabbed the wheel with his cuffed hand, stopping it. "Where is the guard? The one who caught me?"

Veronica wished they would just whisk him away, out of her life forever. But she walked to the side of the chair and knelt to be eye level with Monroe. "What do you need?" she asked.

He turned his head to meet her gaze. It surprised her to see the clear look in his eyes. "Veronica," he whispered, his voice direct and lucid.

She instinctively drew closer to him.

"Keep your eyes open," Monroe said. "Listen for God's voice. It's all around."

"Come on, Sam," the officer said. "You're freaking the lady out."

Veronica stood, and the nurse pushed the chair forward. As the chair reached the door, it struck the wall.

"Watch it!" the cop said.

The nurse turned to face him. "Sorry. Stupid crooked wheels."

"We're trying to get him out of the hospital, not back in."

"I said I was sorry." She turned back toward the patient. "Hold on... where is he?"

Veronica peered past the cops to see the chair was empty.

"He's gone? Find him!"

They each dashed a different direction.

Veronica joined the search, though she believed Monroe was gone. Whether to a clandestine corner of the hospital or to a new mission for heaven, she didn't know. But his voice lingered with her. Listen for God's voice. Something inside her was almost ready to believe it really was all around her.

The End

Repairing Our Forever

By Kristi Woods

To my fellow tool-carriers,
May you put those faith tools to use without hesitation,
strengthened well by the courage of Christ.

As Veronica peered into her rearview mirror, a prick of heat flashed across her neck then surged through her arms to her fingertips. Red and blue lights. Why now?

"I don't have the time or money for this today." Wind from the van's open window skittered across her cheek as she offered an upward plea. "Lord, help me navigate this. Pleeeeease."

She'd made a promise to fix Miss Betty's car, and a late arrival meant her word hung in limbo. The town's plans, too.

And that wouldn't do.

Even more so, she needed the money from today's job to pay rent and prevent an eviction, not a ticket that sunk her deeper into debt. Mr. State Trooper wasn't the one with the deflated bank account because of an unexpected and unwanted divorce.

She gave a squeeze to the steering wheel, which would have choked the life straight out of it had it housed a heartbeat.

"Perfect. Another piece of paper that'll cost me plenty."

Just two hours earlier, "Rock Around the Clock" had woken her, its jingle a sure sign that Miss Betty, a sixty-eight-year-old with two speeds, go and go faster, waited on the other end of the text message.

A sleepy smile had crept onto Veronica's lips. At least this time her grey-haired friend had waited until sunrise to text.

Her hand made its way to the nightstand and fumbled for the phone. Instead, it landed on something cold and hard. She lifted her head past the billowy white of the pillow.

"My toolbox? How'd this get here?" The previous day's oven-like temperatures and packed schedule must have affected her more than she'd realized.

A sticker on the side of the purple box caught her attention. "Garage on the Go." The edges of her lips inched upward at the sight of it as her index finger ran along the outer ridge. "Lord, I'm ready for today. Whatever it may bring."

Beep.

With her groggy thoughts circling around the business and God, she'd forgotten about the text. A quick tap on the screen brought a message to life.

Miss Betty: GOOD MORNING DARLIN'. ☺ GOT A WRENCH? ESSIE WON'T START. CLICKS BUT NO VROOM! VROOM! MISS BETTY IS ☹. TOWN WILL B 2 IF I CAN'T GET THAT CAR 2 GO.

Veronica chuckled. What other senior wrote texts like a teenager? Redbud Springs' favorite woman kept the community rolling, and her pink 1955 Packard 400 too.

Veronica: HAVE WRENCH, WILL TRAVEL.

Miss Betty: GOTTA BE DONE BY NOON. PARADE DOESN'T WAIT.

Veronica: BE OVER ASAP.

Miss Betty: U R A DOLL. THANK U!

The long-awaited annual parade of cars was scheduled for today. The Citizen of Honor rode in the Packard. Always had. She wouldn't let a broken-down car break tradition—or Miss Betty's heart. Plus, this job would provide the funds needed for rent.

A surge of under-the-hood know-how rolled through her. She'd make everything work out. Somehow. She had to.

Veronica hopped out of bed, slid into her jeans, and twisted her long, dark waves into a loose knot on the top of her head. After a quick spritz of her favorite lavender scent, she snatched the toolbox by its handle and raced out the door.

Now that she was on the road, however, a small problem threatened to derail her timetable: the flashing lights behind her.

Tiny rocks crunched under the tires as she eased to the road's shoulder. She held on to a tiny thread of hope that the state highway patrol car would whiz on by.

It pulled in behind her.

Veronica's chest tightened. "Great. Just great." A muted sound echoed as her thumbs tapped on the steering wheel. No telling how long it'd take to fix the Packard. "Please, hurry."

The state trooper's figure grew larger in the side mirror as he approached her window, his wide-brimmed hat shielding his eyes and part of his nose. His medium build and firm-looking arms Gardnered her attention. No wonder since they filled out space in all the right places. Then again, she'd always been a sucker for a man in uniform.

His steady stride spoke with confidence. Of course. He got paid to write tickets, not pay them like her.

"Good morning, ma'am."

"Morning." She purposefully avoided the *good* part. No sense lying when she failed to see anything good about getting pulled over.

"Where you headed to in such a hurry this morning?"

"I'm going into Redbud Springs for work." She was suddenly aware of her sweaty palms. Happened every time she got nervous. She probably had red splotches on her neck, too. They always surfaced at the wrong time. "I've got a job I need to finish this morning. I—I'm headed there now. Garage on the Go." She thumbed toward the back of the van where her business name, bold in a royal purple, was plastered across the side.

"Garage on the Go, eh?"

"You've heard of it?" Maybe a little small talk would land her a warning versus a ticket.

"License and registration, please."

Guess not.

She fumbled with her wallet and produced her license then gathered the registration from the glove box. "Here."

As he reached for the papers, Veronica noticed the sprinkling of freckles interspersed with reddish hairs on his arm. She once knew and loved a man with arms similar to these. Once. But that was then.

"I've heard of Garage on the Go," he said.

Maybe he was up for small talk after all. "You have?" she asked.

"Mm. Just this week, as a matter of fact."

"Oh?" Pride swelled for this new venture. Word sure did get around fast!

"Aunt Betty mentioned it." He tipped his hat upward to reveal familiar blue eyes. "Veronica, it's me. Tate."

Her mouth fell open. The morning's radar included a car repair, not a ripping open of her heart once again by the man she'd once loved.

"It's good to see you." He cocked his head toward her. His smile spanned the canvas of his fair-skinned face, from one clean-shaven dimple to the other.

"Tate Wilson." Hundreds of butterflies took to flight in her stomach, banging against its walls like an angry mob. She hadn't seen Tate since the day he'd left Redbud Springs years earlier to chase his future. Without her. "What are you doing back here?"

"Working." He opened his mouth as if to add more, but then he closed it.

"Oh." Veronica straightened her slouched shoulders and propped back up the invisible wall she'd built when he'd left. With him within arm's reach, it'd be safer. "Miss Betty never mentioned it."

"I asked her not to. Guess she's pretty good at keeping secrets."

"Guess so." Veronica made a mental note to have a little chat with Miss Betty.

Who was he, waltzing back into town as if nothing happened? He'd broken her heart in two, straight down the middle with laser-like precision. Tossed her aside as though their relationship meant as much as a piece of trash. Well, she wasn't trash. Too bad he hadn't felt the same way. If only she could throw a wrench at him. Or would a screwdriver be better?

"Are you going to write me a ticket?" Two cars whizzed by as she stared out the windshield, her hands clutching the steering wheel.

"Do you want me to?"

"What do you think?" She felt her jaw tighten. "But I'm not in charge here. You are." As always, whatever Tate wanted, Tate got. At least as it pertained to their break-up.

"Must be your lucky day." He held her registration and license toward her.

She snatched the documents, careful not to come in contact with his hand. She wasn't about to let him touch her again all because of a traffic stop. She shoved the papers into her purse.

"Listen, Veronica, you forgot to signal back there at Collier." He pointed to the road behind them. "That's all. I'm not going to write you a ticket. Consider this your warning." He leaned in toward the van and gripped the driver's side window ledge. "But you really should signal. It is the law."

The law? Was he lecturing her? Did he forget the law against breaking a woman's heart? A ripple of fire worked through her. She had every right to be upset. He was the one who left.

She caught a whiff of his cologne's familiar woody scent, and her breath hitched. She hadn't smelled that fragrance since he'd uttered, "I'm sorry" and then turned and walked away years earlier, abandoning their relationship for a career.

"Plus, I saw your van and thought I'd let you know I'm back."

"I see."

The anger gave way to a warm surge that flowed through her. He was here. But who knew for how long?

A part of her wanted to tear into him for leaving. The other half desired to unfold the hurt and set aside the barriers she'd erected, whispering in his ear just how much she'd missed him. But what was she thinking? He was probably on a temporary assignment. What if he had a wife, too? That'd be lemon juice in the wound!

She stole a glance at his left hand. No ring. Miss Betty had never mentioned Tate getting married, but then again, Miss Betty tucked Tate's name far away whenever Veronica came near. Was his empty finger an accurate indicator? Did it matter, though? He wouldn't want a divorced woman, and she wasn't willing to risk the hurt again, even if he did.

"I have a job to get to. Watch your toes, Tate. Don't want to run over 'em." After waving him off, she put the van in drive. But when she pulled away, it took everything she had not to look in the rearview mirror. She wouldn't look. Not again.

Okay, maybe.

***

"How's it going, Veronica?" Miss Betty waltzed into the garage just before noon. "Essie running yet?"

"Car's running." She flung a wrench toward the toolbox. "Ready to get her to the parade?"

"Darlin, you betcha!" Miss Betty plopped down in the passenger seat. "How about an ice cream on the way?"

"You're a bad influence on my waistline."

"It's just an itty-bitty cheat. Girls need their ice cream, you know, and it's on me." Her giggle filled the car. "Say, would you do the honor of driving the Packard in the parade?" She checked her watch. "It's almost time. Plus, I'd feel safer knowing you were behind the wheel. You know, just in case the old girl coughs a little and clinks out again." She leaned toward the dashboard and whispered as she gave the car several gentle pats. "Not that I want that, Essie."

"I don't think you'll have any trouble. I fixed her, remember?"

"Yes, but it is an older car." She tapped her chest. "Like us silver-haired folks, sometimes our bodies kink at the least expected times. Don't want Essie to do the same."

"What about Tate?"

Miss Betty's head snapped toward Veronica, and her eyes widened. "Tate? What about him?"

"Well, he's your nephew. Why couldn't he drive Essie?" Veronica studied her friend, searching for any hints her expression might divulge.

"He—he's not available." Her eyebrows raised a little further. "Why?"

Veronica stared at Miss Betty through the narrow slits in her eyes. "Because I saw him this morning."

"Oh." She sank back against the seat, the surprised look softening into a coating of relief. "Is that so?"

"Yes. During a traffic stop."

"What? Tate pulled you over?"

"Sure did." And he'd turned Veronica's world upside down. But Miss Betty didn't need to know that. Neither did Tate.

"No!" Miss Betty gave a little hand slap on her leg. "That little booger."

"Why didn't you tell me? At least let me get prepared?"

"He made me promise."

"I see. Your loyalty to him goes blood deep, much deeper than our friendship."

Miss Betty patted Veronica's arm. "Stop. You know I wouldn't do anything to hurt you or our friendship."

"But you'd keep things from me?" Heat crept up Veronica's neck.

"There was a reason."

The answer lingered in the air, creating more questions for Veronica. "Whatever." Her foot remained on the brake as she pulled on the gear shifter until the car clicked into drive.

"Always did say he let the best fish in the sea get away from him," Miss Betty said.

"Yeah, well, he had different plans in mind. They all do. Men are a finnicky breed." And none of them wanted her.

She wondered why God teased her with relationships that looked good then soured. First Tate, then her ex-husband. She let out a frustration-laced snort.

She'd jumped into a rebound relationship after Tate that had turned into a doomed marriage built on her husband's lies and wandering eyes. No wonder it came crashing down. Maybe she deserved it.

"Have you forgiven him yet?" Miss Betty's question pulled Veronica from her thoughts.

"Who?"

"Tate. Have you forgiven him?"

Sure, she'd tried. But he'd wronged her. And the ache he caused continued to deepen like an infected wound that refused to heal.

"You haven't, have you?" Miss Betty pressed again.

Veronica let out a long sigh, trying to figure out the response that would keep her safe from her friend's prying intuition. "Why do you say that?"

"Because of the look on your face."

Veronica couldn't bring herself to answer. Every muscle inside her screamed she hadn't but needed to.

"Look at it this way." Miss Betty shifted in her seat. "Would you try to be a mechanic without your screwdrivers or wrenches?"

"No."

"It'd be a little difficult to do the job with them lying around, unused, wouldn't it?"

Veronica nodded.

"Oh, sweet one, forgiveness is a God-given tool for His people. It's like the wrench placed in our life's toolbox, ready for a simple or major work. But quite worthless when left unused." She reached over and laid her hand on Veronica's arm then gave a gentle squeeze. "Do you think it's time to pick it up and use it?"

Miss Betty's words swirled in her heart. The scripture about forgiving because she'd been forgiven tagged along too. But could she?

"I'm sorry for not telling you Tate was back in town. Someday, I hope you'll understand why." Miss Betty paused a moment, love swelling in her eyes. "What do you say? Would you do me the honor of driving Essie?"

"I don't have anywhere else to be except on the sidelines, watching from the crowd."

"Pfft! Sidelines are overrated. Besides, you weren't made to stand along the sidelines and watch life pass by. Get in the action. Let's drive!" She gave a little hop in the passenger seat.

Veronica's chuckle swelled into a full-blown smile. She loved this woman like a mother. Not to mention, Miss Betty had raised Tate as her own after his parents died. Her friend would never do anything to hurt her. "If you say so."

"I do." She punched her fist into the air then leaned forward and tapped the dash again. "Essie, Veronica's gonna take real good care of you. Treat her well, you hear?"

"Let's grab some ice cream then make our way to the parade." Veronica slid her foot from the brake as the yumminess of chocolate flirted with her taste buds.

"Yes, let's. Right after we pick up the Redbud Springs Citizen of the Year."

Veronica's eyebrows raised. "We're picking up the Citizen of the Year?"

"We are."

"Who is it?"

Miss Betty made a zipper motion across her lips. "Someone special."

"A current Redbud Springs resident?" She eyed Miss Betty for clues, but the woman's fingers rested on her lips, no hints seeping past them. "Or a past resident?"

"Guess you'll just have to see." She settled her hands on the seat and nodded toward the windshield. "Shall we go?"

"You're not going to tell me?"

"You'll see."

"I'll bet you never shared a secret even as a child, did you? And you probably double wrapped Christmas presents to prevent peeking." She studied Miss Betty's face. "You did, didn't you!"

"Maybe." She winked and pointed toward the road ahead, that warm smile of hers growing. "Onward to Maple Street."

Five minutes later, Miss Betty pointed to a house at the end of the cul-de-sac. "There. That one. Pull up to the white house—the one with the green shutters. Chet Boyd's old place."

Cute home. Veronica wasn't sure who'd purchased it after Mr. Boyd died, but it looked like they took good care of it.

Miss Betty leaned over and gave the horn two short toots then made her way to the front door and rang the bell. The woman knew what she wanted and went after it. That was certain.

Veronica dug her phone from her purse to check her email then got caught up in an online word search game.

She barely noticed when Miss Betty opened the passenger door, rustled around a bit, then slid in.

Without looking, Veronica tossed the phone in her purse. "Ready?"

"More than ready."

She stilled. The voice was far too deep to be Miss Betty's. A thick hand rested on the seat between them. A cross bracelet, copper and well-worn, wrapped around the wrist. She knew that piece of jewelry well. She'd given it. A surge of electricity pulsed through her.

"Tate?" She cocked her head as if one ear could hear the deafening truth staring back at her better than the other. "What are you doing here?"

"Trying to make it to the parade." He crinkled his eyebrows. "They tend to like the Citizen of the Year to be on time."

"What? Citizen of the year? You?"

"Yep. Guess Aunt Betty talked me up to the committee. Besides, they figured it was a good way to let everyone know I was back." His voice softened. "For good."

"For good?"

He nodded.

Was hyperventilating an option? Veronica clutched at her chest, hoping the knee-jerk reaction looked more under-the-wire than Fred Sanford-ish.

He let out a long breath, an exhale that puddled around her heart. "I wanted you to know before everyone else found out."

His words gently encircled her. But why would he care about her now—after all these years?

Just then, the garage door opened, and a car emerged. It pulled up and paused beside the Packard, Miss Betty at the wheel. "We'll get dessert later. It's still on me. See you at the parade! Oh, and don't forget to let me know how much I owe you." She waved and turned onto the street, accelerating in the parade's direction before Veronica could corral her thoughts to make sense of everything.

"Miss Betty!" Veronica called after her. "Where are you going?"

"Pretty sure she didn't hear you, but she said she'd see you at the parade." Tate's lips curved into an ornery grin.

"Don't be smug."

"It's what she said." He shrugged as he thumbed toward Miss Betty's car. His grin widened.

"Did you change your mind? Are you going to give me a ticket after all?" Was that an edge to her words? Probably. Did it matter? Probably not. Tate always could see straight through her.

"No. This isn't about a ticket. Far from it." He fingered her sleeve. "It's about you. And me." He cleared his throat. "It may not seem like it, but I've missed you."

Veronica snorted and yanked back. "You're right. It hasn't seemed that way."

"But it's true." He rotated his bracelet around his wrist.

"What about the text you didn't answer?"

"Text?" His head cocked. "I didn't get a text."

"Likely story. I sent one on your birthday right after we broke up." She'd desperately missed him, and his birthday had provided a perfect excuse to reach out. But he didn't reach back. That's when she knew there'd be no reviving of their relationship.

He sucked in a deep breath. "I changed my number."

Their conversation tossed her like a lost soul out in the middle of an angry ocean. "Figures."

"Not because of you. Some advertisement for pillows listed my number by accident. I kept getting calls to order the Sound Z's Tonight special. Big pain. So, I changed my number."

"You missed me, but it never occurred to you to let me know?" A pillow advertisement had robbed her of her future? Maybe he should have thought up a better story!

"It happened a few weeks after we broke up. It didn't make sense to let you know."

"You're the one who took the assignment on the other side of the state." The one who chose a career over her. She looked out the side window. "Congratulations, Trooper Wilson. You got what you wanted."

"Veronica, come on. Don't do this." He leaned in closer.

"Do what? I promised to drive your aunt's car today, and that's precisely what I'll do. Of course, I had no idea you'd be in it, but I'll keep my word. She's important to me. So is the town." Veronica rolled her eyes. "Unlike other people in this car."

"Aunt Betty's important to me, too. And the town. But especially you."

She released a deep sigh that took years of breath with it. "Whatever."

"I never forgot you. Never. When I realized my huge mistake by letting you go, I came back for you. Even had the ring."

"Ring?"

"Ring."

The lump in Veronica's throat doubled in size.

"Finally realized how wrong I was to marry my job and not the love of my life. I came back as soon as I could, hoping you'd take me back."

"But you never came."

His voice lowered. "That was the weekend you eloped."

Veronica's head dropped. "Oh." Pain, like she'd heard in his voice, raked across her heart.

Tate had come back for her, and she'd missed him. It felt like a punch in the gut.

"Once you married, it would have been wrong for me to be in your life. You and I both know that." His Adam's apple dipped, and after a pause, he continued. "It was too painful to stand by and watch, so I left. Again. Threw myself into work to take my mind off you." He gave a half-hearted laugh. "It didn't work."

He reached toward her. His touch noticeably warm after cutting through the frozen tundra between them. "Please forgive me for ever letting you go."

Could she? She'd tried for years without success.

Forgive as you've been forgiven.

"Even though you'd moved on, I never married." He looked out the window then swiveled back toward Veronica. "Guess I never got over you."

Was that a tear puddling in the corner of his eye?

"Veronica, I'll always love you. That's just the way it is. But if you can't forgive me, I understand."

She buried her head in her hands, tears dripping from her eyes. He loved her. Still. All this time, and she never knew. "Don't say that."

"Why?"

"Because. It's too late. Trust me, you don't want this." She lifted her head and motioned toward herself. "I'm a divorced woman. A marriage throwaway."

"Don't say that." He wiped her cheek of moisture. "Let me be the one who wipes away your tears, not causes more of them. The one who helps bring smiles and laughter. The one who's privileged to live with you. Forever."

Through the blur of tears, she studied his eyes. "Why should I believe you?"

"Have I ever lied to you?"

He hadn't. He was a man of his word—one thing Veronica liked most about him. One of the hardest things to let go of, too.

"Give me another chance," Tate said. "Will you?"

He reached for her hand and pulled it to his cheek, cradling her in the safety of his touch. Then, he lifted her hand to his lips, gracing her skin with a gentle kiss that warmed her like nothing had in a long, long time.

"I'm scared," she whispered. "I always dreamed you'd return, but then you didn't. And it hurt." She grabbed at her chest and another tear dropped.

Forgive as you have been forgiven.

"I'm sorry." With a gentle swipe, he captured a tear as it traveled down her cheek.

The situation felt like the Tilt-a-Whirl ride at the fair. Around and around, clutching the bar yet feeling as though she were about to fly off the seat. Dizzying views of life circling and about to swallow her.

Forgive as you have been forgiven.

"I want to." She stared down at her hands. "But it's hard."

Had she offered the words to Tate or God? Maybe both? Did it matter? She'd wrestled with forgiving him for a long time. Far too long. Did she really want to keep living like that?

She'd been given the tools, yet her spiritual toolbox remained closed concerning Tate and forgiveness. Was it time to click the latch and open it?

At that moment, something familiar tugged at her heart. It was time to let go of the hurt and trust God instead. Even if she was scared.

"Tate Wilson," she whispered, "I forgive you."

And she meant it.

With three forced-out words that had been dammed up inside of her for far too long, Veronica smashed the off button, and hurt's dizzying ride came to a halt. She'd carried the tool of forgiveness all along. She simply needed to put it to use.

The gleam in Tate's eyes brightened. "You do?"

She nodded.

"You've just made me a happy man, Veronica." Relief echoed in his words. "A very happy man. But one more question."

"Hm?"

"Will you take a chance on love again?" He cleared his throat and shifted in his seat. "With me?"

She'd never seen him that uneasy before as he shifted in his seat. He'd put it all out on the line. For her.

"Maybe," she said.

His eyes widened as his grin faded into two straight lines. "Maybe? What does that mean?"

The corners of her lips curved upward as she wagged a finger at him. "No more pulling me over, mister."

"You might persuade me, if you follow the law." His soft laugh filtered into the air.

"Tate!" She socked him with a playful touch.

He grabbed her arm, leaned over, and pulled her into his warm embrace. Then he eased his hands to her cheeks, cradling them as he peered into her eyes. Her muscles turned to jelly.

"I never want to lose you again, Veronica."

He closed the distance between them, the salty taste of his lips grazing across hers with a gentleness that had been absent for far too long. Tate paused as though waiting for permission, then pressed deeper into the kiss. Not a single muscle in her body protested.

"Not you or your purple toolbox," he mouthed against her lips.

She pulled back and pressed her forehead to his, the tips of their noses touching. "I never wanted to lose you. Can we go slow?"

"You have my word."

Maybe looking in the rearview mirror wasn't so bad after all. What they saw in theirs might help them build a better future.

"Time to repair our forever, Tate Wilson."

"It's time." He pressed his lips to her hand, and a tidal wave of warm tingles washed over her. "I could stay here with you forever."

"Me too."

"But we have a parade and town waiting on us."

She sighed. "Not to mention Miss Betty."

"Yes, and Aunt Betty." He squeezed Veronica's hand. "What do you say? Be my ride?"

"Now that our citizen of the year is finally back where he belongs? You betcha. Forever." She gave his hand a return squeeze then pulled the Packard's shifter into gear.

THE END

Author's Note:

I hope you enjoyed this short story. Within it lives a question each of us faces in our lifetime: How do (or should) I forgive? It often seems difficult. And let's be honest, sometimes we simply don't want to! Refusing forgiveness, however, lands us in darkness's playground. This is a spiritual battle, after all. Do we really want to ride the merry-go-round?

Truth be told, I don't. How about you?

By resting in God's faithfulness and leaning on His truth through scriptures such as Ephesians 4:32, we know we're called to forgive. And we can, no matter how difficult it seems.

If you're wrestling with forgiveness today concerning a loved one, a friend, or someone else, will you hunker in and offer forgiveness?

I've placed a prayer and a few helpful tools, including my story and struggle with forgiveness, at this link:

https://kristiwoods.net/how-the-power-of-forgiveness-can-help-you/

A special thanks to author and friend Jennifer Slattery for your suggestions—at the last minute! God's using you.

A huge thanks to my husband, Tony, and children Joel, Beka, and Caleb. Your patience, listening ears, and cheerleading mean the world to me.

As for the KristiWoods.net subscribers who volunteered their reading and feedback skills, thank you. You helped make this a stronger story.

Last but most important, I couldn't do this without You, my Father. Thank You. May You be glorified.

The Letter in the Garden

By Bill Garrison

The yard still hadn't recovered from the weather.

Ahhh, the Oklahoma weather. The ice storm before Halloween, the resulting power outage, the blizzard that would make Alaskans proud... Certainly, a year to remember. But did she remember it? Really remember it?

What did it matter? Veronica Wilson knew that today, a warm spring day with a shining sun and a slight breeze, she had a yard to clean.

Aside from making her wear her jacket on an otherwise warm day, the wind helped by blowing most of the trash flush against the south fence in her back yard. She was on her second bag of trash when she saw a piece of paper fluttering amid the debris. It didn't look like a letter at first, just a folder piece of paper, but she picked it up and saw all the clean cursive handwriting. And then she noticed the date.

July 14, 1994

Magnum,

I hope you are having a good summer. I know it didn't turn out like we had hoped. Working at Camp Bond with you would have been so much fun. The camp brings back so many great memories of my childhood, and I know you'll be making good memories for all the children you get to meet and teach this summer.

I wanted to tell you this in person, but it's almost impossible with your schedule and I won't be back to Oklahoma until the first of August.

Joseph came back, and we are dating again.

There, I said it. I am so so so so so so sorry.

I know you're hurt and have so many questions.

I wasn't lying to you when I told you I thought I would never see him again. With his dad's job, Joseph and I knew he might be moving when we started dating but we didn't know he would leave over spring break. It was so sudden. I once again thank you for giving me the space I needed. I didn't expect to fall in love with you, but I did. And I did love you. Still do. Always will.

Anyway. Joseph's parents got divorced, and his mom moved back to Oklahoma City. And he came with her. He just knocked on my door a few days after you left for the summer. At first, we just talked but my heart was so heavy because he and I had broken up for reasons out of my control. I still loved him.

And...well, you don't need to know the rest. But we decided to get back together.

That's not the worst part.

I just found out I'm pregnant.

I am wiping tears away as I write this. I didn't want this. I didn't plan this. I feel like I have let so many people down. Yet, here I am. Pregnant and afraid. Jenny has been here for me since the beginning. You remember Jenny? Jenny Weissman? I haven't told Joseph yet. Jenny thinks I should tell him YESTERDAY. But I wanted to tell you first.

I feel like I have ruined everything. My relationship with you, my relationship with Joseph, my relationship with God, and my future. I really wish you....

Veronica read with her mouth open. What a fascinating and tragic story. She turned the page, and...nothing. Blank. No more. Where was the rest? She wanted to know more. Who wrote this tragically sad letter. And how did it end up in her yard? Who was the father of this baby? Magnum, probably. But, could be Joseph.

"Mom, are you OK?"

She turned to her son, Cory, who'd stepped onto the back porch.

She chuckled. "Sorry, I found this crazy letter in the garden."

"You looked like a statue."

"The letter is interesting, to say the least. How was practice?"

"Bad. Coach is still angry we lost."

Veronica nodded. She knew the drill. Losing had a price.

"I'm gonna go get my haircut," Cory said. "Tell me about the letter at dinner?"

"Sure." She waved, but he was already back inside.

That night, they ate homemade enchiladas while Cory read the letter. When he was done, he looked at his mom, wide-eyed. "Is this real?"

"I think so," Veronica said. "I have no reason to think it isn't."

"It can't be twenty years old. It looks to be in good condition. Almost new."

"I thought so too. The paper is a little wrinkled and dirty, but I don't think it's been rained on."

Through a mouthful of food, Cory said, "So, an old letter recently found a home in your garden."

Veronica frowned. "Or maybe the date is wrong."

"Do people even write letters like that anymore?"

Veronica shook her head. "No. Text, email, social media. College kids would do anything before writing and mailing an actual letter. I don't know how, but this letter hasn't been in my garden long."

They talked about it for a few more minutes, and then Cory left to hang out with some friends.

They'd moved to a new city, and though Veronica hadn't met many people, Cory slipped right into the new school district, which had been a blessing from God. He fit right in and immediately made friends. He played on the basketball team, logging enough time to keep him happy. But Veronica's nightly routine remained the same, no matter where they lived. It wouldn't always be like this. When you hit rock bottom, it takes a while to climb out. Her husband's death had left her empty.

She watched a little TV. Made a cake. Cleaned up. Took a warm bath with a Jennifer Weiner novel in hand. Then climbed under the covers at ten thirty, knowing Cory would be home in thirty minutes.

In bed with the lights out and her AirPods on, she selected her *Robert Earl Keen* playlist and let her mind drift. Memories of her friends and crazy jobs she had a bridesmaid, a mechanic, and a hospital guard. Good memories. She whispered a prayer for Cory.

Thank you, God, for being there for him during this move and transition and for everything going so seamlessly.

God, please be with me as I transition into this new stage in life.

Thoughts of grocery lists and weekend plans drifted into her head and became jumbled with silly thoughts that only come when she was near sleep.

The letter.

Suddenly wide awake, she thought about the letter. The writer had poured her heart out to a guy name Magnum, and somehow the letter had ended up in Veronica's backyard. How did the letter end? Did she end up telling Magnum he was the father, or did she let him know it was Joseph? It didn't really matter to her life, yet something inside her urged her to do more.

***

In between jobs, Veronica didn't have to worry about getting ready for...well, anything. She woke before seven and made her bed and then had breakfast with Cory. After he left for school, she put on leggings and a light fleece jacket and set out for a morning jog on the cool February day.

She enjoyed running in her new neighborhood. The diverse mixture of houses meant no run seemed the same. On one street, she saw dilapidated houses next to brand new condos and mid-century houses next to brick bungalows over a century old.

She kept to the shoulder, dodging the occasional car and nodding at neighbors in their yards. Up ahead, a girl came her way. She wore jeans and a hoodie with headphone wires running to the pockets.

The girl seemed oblivious, lost in her own world and walking at a leisurely pace. As Veronica got closer, she surmised the girl to be sixteen or seventeen. She had long straight black hair that flowed out of her hood and down over her shoulders. The girl didn't even look up when Veronica jogged past her on the other side of the road.

A white truck was parked at the next corner. A man sat in the front seat and blew cigarette smoke through a cracked window. He wore a denim work shirt and had black wavy shoulder length. His gaze focused on something beyond Veronica. A house? The girl?

Then he snapped out of it, made brief eye contact with Veronica, and drove away.

Weird. Interesting.

The street angled downhill, which meant the trip back up would be arduous. She passed one of her favorite houses, a red brick bungalow with a beautiful rose garden in the front. "Exes and Oh's" by Elle King came on her playlist and she smiled at a memory. A few years ago in a half marathon, her MP3 player got stuck on this song. She hadn't been able to change it without slowing her pace, so she just listened to the song over and over....and over.

Five minutes later, she turned a corner and reached her street. The home stretch. Her hamstrings ached and her lungs burned. One final block and she would be done for the day.

Several houses in front of her was the hooded girl she had seen before. The truck with the creepy guy slowly kept pace. The girl turned her head towards the pickup, then turned away and put her head down.

Was that guy talking to her? Did he know her?

The girl didn't look like she wanted to talk.

Veronica sped up, ignoring her body's protests. Five houses away, then four. Then the brake lights on the truck flashed, and it moved away from the curb and turned left at the next street. Had he seen Veronica in his rear-view mirror? Why pull away if he wasn't doing anything wrong?

The girl turned as Veronica approached.

"Was that man bothering you?" Veronica asked as she stopped beside the teenager.

"No."

"Are you sure?"

"He's just doing what he always does?"

"And what's that?"

"Being a...well, a jerk."

"Sounds like he was bothering you."

The girl kept walking. "It's no big deal. He works for the college. He has a reputation."

The college was a few blocks east, sharing a square mile with the high school.

"I am home." The girl turned left and went into a house with sagging window air conditioners and fading and flaking white paint.

Veronica stood for a moment then jogged home. While taking a shower, she thought about the girl and the guy in the truck and wondered if she should do anything about it.

Later that day, Veronica got on her laptop to find Jenny Weisman, the friend the letter writer had referred to. Veronica found a woman with that name on Facebook who lived in Oklahoma City. They had one mutual friend, Will Martin, Cory's coach. This could be the Jenny Weisman referenced in the letter. She sent Jenny a friend request a long with a message about a question she needed to ask her.

***

Veronica showed up at the high school at four thirty. She wore black leggings and a forest green fleece. Her wardrobe didn't vary much these days.

A group of moms had planned to meet at the school after practice to decorate the locker room before Friday's homecoming game.

Veronica was walking along the corridors when she passed an office door on her right and she heard someone call her name. She stopped and stuck her head in. Coach Martin sat at his desk. He wore a dri-fit school shirt and a Nike baseball cap covered his dark wavy hair.

Her stomach fluttered just a bit. "Hi, coach."

"Come on in for a second."

She stepped into the large office, which had a flat screen TV and a bookshelf lined with books and trophies on one wall. Another wall had various photos from the coach's career. Coach Martin had played at an NCAA Division 2 school in the 1990s and then played professionally in Europe for a few years before getting into coaching.

"Yes?"

"Just wanted to say hello," he said.

She smiled. "You're having a great season, and Cory's having lots of fun."

"Thank you. And Cory's doing great. I know it's hard for kids to move to a new school, but he works hard."

"I appreciate you saying that." None of the pictures included Coach with another woman. Veronica knew he wasn't married, and maybe he wasn't dating either.

They talked for a few minutes about the decorating the moms would be doing in the locker room. She should be helping the moms but didn't want to leave. The only other time she had talked to him for any amount of time was at the pancake breakfast fundraiser last November.

"Well," she said, "I guess I'd better—"

"Would you like to go out to dinner with me?"

"Sure," she said quickly. Too quickly?

"After the season, of course. So, it might be a month or so. But I wanted to ask you now."

"Of course. After the season. Here, let me give you my number so we can talk more." She took a pen and post-it note off the front of his desk and jotted her number down. "I should join the other moms in the locker room."

"Let me apologize in advance for the smell."

She laughed. "No need. One teenage boy, or fifteen. The smell is bad."

Standing by the door, she pointed to a picture on the wall. "So, you won a national championship?"

"Won one and almost another. I never thought I would be back so close to where I went to college."

She tapped one of the photos. "I love your mustache. Didn't that go out of style a decade or two before you played?"

Coach Martin laughed. "Oh man, the guys gave me a hard time about that. They called me 'Magnum.'"

A jolt shot through Veronica's body.

"You know, after Tom Selleck...Magnum PI."

"I've heard of it."

"Thankfully, it was a short-lived phase," he said. "Again, thank you for helping with the locker rooms. I'll text you later."

The entire time she helped decorate the locker room, she thought about Coach Martin, most likely the "Magnum" in the letter from the garden. Either he found out he was a father from that letter, or that his ex was having a baby with another man. Did it matter that he was the man? Did it matter who Joseph was, or Jenny Weisman, or the writer of the letter? While the letter certainly piqued her interest and initially seemed like a mystery that needed solving, now that she knew one of the players in the drama, it seemed less necessary. Most likely everyone involved in the letter knew everything anyway, and certainly way more than she knew.

***

Coach texted her on Thursday night, and they chatted a little bit about basketball and their kids but nothing serious.

Friday night for homecoming, Veronica wore her gray hoodie with the team mascot on the front. She worked the concession stand for the girl's game and then found her normal place next to two other single moms, whose kids played on JV.

After the game, she joined the other parents waiting for the boys to come out of the locker room. She stood next to a couple. The mom wore jeans and a school hoodie while the dad looked like he came straight from the office, with slacks, a white dress shirt, and a loosened tie hanging from his neck. The mom said, "Cory played a great game. He hit some big shots."

"Thank you." Veronica never tired of people complimenting her son.

"I'm sorry I didn't introduce myself the other night when we decorated the lockers. My name is Isabel and this is my husband Joseph."

He stepped forward. "Call me Joe." He shook her hand.

Joseph? Could this be the Joseph in the letter? "I'm sorry, but which one is your son?"

"He's Brennan," said Isabel.

Veronica nodded. The starting point guard. "He played a great game," she said. "Really kept the team together." Brennan would be too young to be the one referenced in the letter.

A girl approached them. She had straight long hair and a fair complexion with freckles dotting her nose and cheeks.

"This is our daughter Maddie. She's a sophomore in college," Joseph said.

Veronica smiled at the cute girl and realized she could be the exact age of the baby in the letter.

The conversation continued along normal topics. The officiating. The upcoming opponents. Chances to make the state tournament. But inside, Veronica recalled the pictures in Coach Martin's office. No other children but his son in high school, who also played on the team. Or did she just miss it?

Since the page of the letter she had didn't say who the father was, there could only be two options. Either Coach Martin wasn't the father, or Coach Martin didn't know he had a daughter. If he had a daughter he didn't know about, should she be the one to tell him? Or one last option, maybe everyone knew everything and Veronica needed to not worry about it.

Veronica shook her head. This was stupid. Tomorrow, she would show Coach Martin the letter and find out what really happened.

After going out to IHOP with some of the other parents, it was nearly midnight when she reached her neighborhood. Thanks to homecoming, people walked the streets and cars came and went. The town came alive on a Friday night, and even more because of homecoming.

She stopped at a stop sign. Two houses down, a hatchback had just parked on the right side of the road, facing Veronica. With its headlights still on, she couldn't see the driver. A white full-size cargo van crept slowly down the street towards her and was almost even with the parked car.

Its headlights were off. Why?

The driver of the van, a woman. The passenger, a man with black wavy shoulder-length hair, smoking a cigarette filling the cabin with smoke.

The girl opened her car door and got out. It was Maddie, Joseph and Isabel's daughter.

With a roar of the engine, the van leapt forward and stopped with a shudder. The man jumped out of the front passenger seat, slid the cargo door open, and wrapped his arms around the girl in a bear hug.

He wrangled her off the ground and almost did a dive into the back of the van.

Before they even landed, the van's engine roared again, and the van sprung forward, its tires screeching.

The people in the van were kidnapping that girl! Veronica stepped on her gas, her sedan burst forward and rammed into the van.

Veronica's air bag exploded. She had braced for it and shook off the blow and exited her SUV in one fluid motion.

The van's windshield had shattered, shards of glass spread across its dashboard and the pavement. The van's driver sat in a stunned gaze, then in a panic tried to unfasten her seatbelt.

The sliding cargo door was wide open, and the stunned girl sat with wide eyes. Where was the man that took her? Veronica looked to her left, then right and saw him running up the street.

"Maddie, are you ok?"

"He…just grabbed me…and then…"

"Maddie!" It was her dad, Joseph. He sprinted from his front yard, with Isabel not far behind. Maddie would be ok.

Veronica left he scene and sprinted after the kidnapper. The man ran, but Veronica gained on him. He turned a corner, but she kept gaining.

"Stop," she yelled.

Suddenly the man stopped and turned to face her. He bent at the knees, breathing heavy and hard. His right hand brandished a knife. He swore at her.

Veronica rushed him. This seemed to startle him. He took a swing, which she easily deflected, and then she threw a punch that cracked his nose. She heard the crunch, and the blood began pouring out. He screamed in pain.

She grabbed the arm of his knife hand and twisted until the knife fell, then with a leg sweep, knocked his legs out from under him and pushed him onto his stomach on the ground. She kneeled on top of him and held his left arm behind his back. She pulled out her phone and called the police with her other hand.

By the time a patrol car arrived, a small crowd had gathered around her. Two police officers cuffed the man and read him his rights.

After talking with a detective named Simmons for a few minutes, she walked back with him back to the scene of the wreck and kidnapping. There, she spent another hour talking to the police, and along with Maddie, telling her story. She mentioned the girl she saw the other day being stalked by the same man and told them where she lived.

"Maddie!" a man shouted from up the street.

Veronica turned to see Coach Will Martin sprinting towards Maddie.

"Dad!" Maddie met him in an embrace in the middle of the street. She sobbed into his arms.

Apparently, Will did know about Maddie. He was her father. Joseph must be her stepdad, and Isabel the writer of the letter. Veronica breathed a sigh of relief. Everyone knew what they needed to know. Thank God she hadn't stuck her nose into what the letter said. But also, thank God she had noticed the guy in the van and been there when Maddie needed her. No telling what would have happened if the cargo van had gotten away.

Coach Martin and Maddie approached Veronica. He pulled her into a hug. "Thank you for saving Maddie," he whispered. "Thank you for being there."

When he pulled away, she could see the pain and fear in the redness of his eyes and the tears on his face.

"I'm so glad I was here."

Detective Simmons approached and spoke to Maddie. "Here is my card. We will be talking with you a little bit more."

Then he turned to Veronica. "Thank you for what you did tonight."

"Your welcome," she said. "Thank you for your service, Major Simmons."

"And thank you for your service as well, Sergeant Wilson."

Coach Martin's eyes widened. "What? I didn't know you were in the military."

"I was," Veronica said with a smile. "And boy do I have some stories to tell."

Lock down! This is Real.

By Katherine Webster

Asami's petite body lay next to Veronica on the classroom floor. Lifeless!

Veronica tried to piece together what had happened. Why could she not remember? Her hand closed around her gun. Was she a murderer?

Police and her students gathered around them. Her memory flashed back to that morning, to the principal's frantic shouting. "School Lockdown. This is Real!"

7:00 am

Veronica opened the heavy school doors. On the second floor, she glanced at the Anti-Muslim graffiti on the wall. Her Muslim students were still being targeted as terrorists.

She opened the classroom door and sat at a wooden desk. Everything looked familiar from last semester. A geography poster and history timeline hung on the wall. An American flag, a government poster, and a small, framed US Constitution were behind her desk.

"We are so glad you chose Chisholm school Veronica!" Principal Trenton stepped into the room. "You are so creative and patient with your students."

"Thanks," said Veronica. A small ESL history class. The perfect teaching job for her. Being small framed she did not want to manage a class of forty kids. She wanted to teach her students to read on a 9th-grade level and when they were seniors they could be in regular classes.

8:30 am

When the first bell rang, she tapped on the computer to take roll, but the screen was blank. She tapped the screen again. Blank! She panicked.

Jorge her soft cheeked Mexican student laughed. "I think you need to plug in the computer."

"Thanks, Jorge." After the computer booted up, she began. "Hello 9th graders, my name is Ms. Wilson, and I am your ELS history teacher. When I call your name say, 'Here' and I will not mark you absent today."

The students looked relieved. They started the routine of Monday's History class.

Helga, the blond-haired, Bulgarian girl sitting in the first row jumped up immediately and came to Veronica's desk. "Do you need zum help to take the roll?" she asked in her thick Bulgarian accent.

"Thank you," said Veronica.

Helga had come from a Bulgarian orphanage and was adopted by American parents. Helga was now her teacher's pet!

Veronica put the 5-minute warm-up question on the screen when the loud megaphone speaker in the corner vibrated the morning announcements from Principal Trenton.

"Good morning students. Let's begin with a moment of silence."

The class stilled.

"Please stand to say the Pledge of Allegiance."

Veronica crossed her arm over her chest, and she looked at the American Flag. She would teach her students about citizenship and the government of the United States this year. The class recited the pledge of allegiance in broken English.

After the announcements. Veronica began her lessons on the whiteboard. "Who can pick the correct answer? What are the 3 parts of the United States government?

1. Executive, Legislative, Judicial.

2. Executive, Judicial. House of representatives.

3. Financial, President, Speaker of the house.

Jorge wiggled his arm in the air. "I know the answer." At her go-ahead, he said, "It is number 1 Executive, Legislative, Judicial."

"Correct!" said Veronica. "Can you find an example of this in the government?"

The kids knew more than she'd anticipated, and she was pleased to see how well they were absorbing the information she was teaching.

These students came from countries run by terrorism, poverty, and dictatorships. They'd come to live the American dream of freedom. She had read their student files. Jorge was 15 an illegal immigrant from Mexico. He and his mother had traveled two thousand miles from Acapulco to escape the

Cartel that killed his grandparents, father, and his two sisters. They arrived in the United States with nothing, but they would not be targeted by the Cartel.

Asami and Mohammad came to America to escape terrorism, war, and religious persecution. The Taliban had ruined their country and people were starving. Their mother had met an American soldier and married him to escape religious persecution. Asami was very shy, but polite. She was on Level 2 in her speaking and reading. Her brother Mohammad was tall and very handsome. He was on Level 5 in English. He was very protective of his sister, Asami.

The Yang family came from China to escape communism. Kim's parents found good jobs in the US. Kim Yang was on Level 3 in English, but his speaking was level 1.

Veronica had a heart for immigrants from all countries. She knew that even though we may look and speak differently, we are all the same. Her goal was to raise their English level to five so they could go to regular classes by their senior year.

9:17 am

Suddenly alarms began blaring from the speaker in the corner.

The principal voice was urgent but calm "This is a Lockdown!! There is a Shooter in the building."

Veronica trembled with fear. She felt shocked and frozen. But the sound of gunshots nearby jarred her out of her stupor.

The students covered their ears. They smelled the gunfire and saw the smoke in the hall.

She focused on them, she saw wide eyes and dropped jaws!

"Ms. Wilson I am scared!" Kim's voice rose, and he pulled out his phone and began tapping on the screen.

"Turn off your phones and be silent," Veronica put her finger to her lips.

"What is a Lock down?" asked Jorge.

"It is when a shooter has gotten into the school building. We must lock our doors and go into hiding. I will protect you."

Veronica knew the shooter had a perfect shot through the window of her classroom door.

She read the emergency drill procedure for lock-down. "Lock all doors and windows immediately. If a door cannot be locked block the door with heavy items. Always ask for documentation from officials to confirm their identity.

Turn off all lights and close the blinds. Stay low and away from the windows and doors. Stay in the classroom. Turn off cell phones and other electronics."

She focused on Jorge, who watched her with an eerie calm. "Check that the door is locked."

He nodded and hurried to it.

"Helga, cover the window with cardboard and tape!"

The girl stared at her, wide-eyed.

"Hurry!" Veronica snapped. She must hide her students from the shooter.

"We need to get out of this classroom. Let's go into the teacher's closet." She commanded her scared students to follow her into the five by ten closet, and she locked the heavy door behind them. Her fifteen students stood frozen against the wall in the small area. "Let's sit down and breathe. We are safe. Let's pray together for our safety."

The group began saying our father.

Veronica continued praying "Lord of power protect all of us today. Keep us away from the anger of the shooter. Pray that he will be stopped."

Helga prayed the Hail Mary with her Rosary beads. Jorge was on his knees praying and bowing. The four Venezuelan girls were crying from fear.

"Who can protect us? There are no police officers here." said Esperanza.

Veronica gave them a hug. "We will survive."

Asami whispered to her brother in Farci "The shooter wants to kill us because we are Muslims."

The classroom door slammed open. Had someone kicked it in? Footsteps stomped toward the closet. Someone pounded on the closet door.

"Where are Asami and Mohammad? Who is in the closet?"

Veronica slowly got her gun from the safe in the closet. She had been trained in gun safety but had never had to use it in school.

The banging continued. Veronica pointed, "Climb up the ladder and hide on the roof. You will be safe."

The lock shattered after a gunshot and the shooter stepped into the teacher's closet. Veronica pointed her gun at the shooter.

"No more killing," Veronica yelled. "This stops now."

She heard a gunshot from her classroom, the shooter fell. At the same time, a loud crash came from behind her.

Police rushed in, hauling the shooter away. Veronica turned to see Asami laying on the floor with blood running down her forehead. She must have fallen from the ladder. Veronica sat down feeling for a pulse. Strong. Asami was just unconscious.

No one else was hurt. The police knelt checking everyone.

10:41 am

"You are safe. The shooter has been caught and sits handcuffed in a police car." The speaker announced. "All students may leave through the auditorium doors."

Mrs. Wilson began walking her foreign students down the stairs to the auditorium. They were tired, confused, and hungry.

"I can't believe this happened in the United States." cried Mohammed cuddling his sister close.

All students began running through the large open doors of the auditorium. Police had ambulances waiting to take the students to the hospital or give medical aid. Parents were waiting behind the gate yelling their child's name.

"Helga, are you safe?" screamed her mom from outside the stadium.

***

As students lit candles, the chaplain spoke "America is a melting pot where immigrants come to escape poverty, dictatorship and war. Being against a race and not knowing students as individuals is Racism."

Veronica and her students authored a poem about the experience and had Helga read it during the Memorial.

> *We are all different but the same*
> *We are Americans who dream of Peace*
> *This will not happen when we hate a race*
> *Past mistakes must be forgiven*
> *Killing is not the answer and never in a school*
> *I pray we'll find our similarities and accept our differences.*

Author's note:

Information to recognize school shooters always "show signs" before they enact their "big and memorable" horrific actions. They have high dysfunctional family situations, no friends, no ethics or values, and they are obsessed with weapons.

Black Wing Angel

By Chris Tarpley

The dripping fog of late evening swirled about the tiny, weed-choked atrium, caressing Veronica's hair like an abusive lover. She pushed a straight black lock over an ear, and it clung to her head. She shifted on her feet, keeping a low crouch in front of the broken glass window, stained brown from some unremembered defilement.

It was the life of a private eye—stale take-out, cramped legs, and the grimiest floors she had ever had the displeasure of knowing. A chopper thrummed overhead like an angel with a rusty flashlight, casting its pale-yellow light on the tall walls above her. The search beams never penetrated down to the ground in this part of the city, where the cockroaches crawled without fear.

She heard muffled voices from a room beyond the broken window, the words spoken too quickly to make out. She pressed her ear as close as she dared to the jagged opening in the dirty glass. An hour ago, she had hidden in the little room, which had only one exit, waiting for her targets to arrive. It was a risk she would never have taken under ordinary circumstances. From what her sources told her, tonight would be the night of the most critical meeting between underworld powers in a generation. Something called the Black Wing Angel was going to be exchanged. Rumors placed it as some horrible new street drug, but nobody knew for sure. All the hard work, the careful planning, and the laying of threads would finally come to a close. A cold-forged steel bear trap was about to snap shut on the legs of the Lucianni crime family.

The last five years had aged her. In her late forties, she barely recognized her reflection in the mirror. It wasn't due to the spots and distortions in the cheap glass that leaned loose above the sink back in her office. She closed her eyes and groaned inside, remembering the life she had left behind. She had a nice, quiet teaching gig, in a good neighborhood, a son who had gotten into a good college, and a blossoming relationship with his former high school coach. Then, she tried to help one of her students who was in trouble. She just had to go and get involved. When the whole stinking trail of corruption led to the door of a federal prosecutor, the life she knew disappeared like a blind date with an empty wallet.

The only thing that kept Veronica from winding up as a Jane Doe in a dust-covered filing cabinet was an ally in a different office. Mr. Bradley was the reason she was alive and now crawling among the same cockroaches. If Mr. Bradley was the shiny red apple, she was the worm hidden inside to surprise the gangster who was about to bite.

She had relocated, given up her name, her old life, and even her connection to her family. Mr Bradley promised she could have it all back after tonight, after their death-stroke against the mob.

Her left leg quivered, and she tried to shift and relieve the stress of a half hour of crouching. It did no good. She placed her handbag on the ground and pulled out a small jar of cream. Quietly unscrewing the lid, she massaged the soothing gel on her aching thigh. Once the mobsters completed their initial patrol of the site, she could relax a bit. It had to be soon.

Glass crunched behind her, and she snatched her purse, twisting upright. She groaned and grasped her left leg as it spasmed from the sudden action, but her mind was focused on the mountain of a man who blocked her only exit from the room. He said nothing, but the cold clack of the hammer on the Colt Python .357 revolver that shined from the middle of his bulk spoke for him.

The man called over his shoulder, "Hey boss! We got ourselves an alley cat prowling where she don't belong." He cocked his head toward the voices in the other room without taking his eyes off her.

They stopped talking. She was trapped, cornered like a mangy dock rat.

Quick, accented words from the other room. The man scratched the side of his head with a catcher's mitt of a hand. "No, uh. I mean, it's a lady."

She ran through her options. There weren't many. In another life, under a different command, she could've called an entire squad of uniforms down on their heads. She considered feinting to one side, trying to duck under his arms and break through to the exit. Her leg twitched, reminding her of the folly of such foolish action. The barrel of that gun was a cyclops daring her to a staring contest she could only lose. What if they decided to just kill her, on the spot? No loose ends. Not even a Jane Doe in a forgotten file. She closed her eyes, not ready, her work unfinished.

"Yeah, boss." The gorilla at the door cracked a toothy grin. "She'll come quietly." He drew his weapon down on her, pressing the circle of cold steel into her forehead and forced her to her knees. She was too relieved at the absence of hot lead in her brain to protest beyond a squawk as he enveloped her slender wrist in his meaty paw.

Veronica recovered her thoughts quickly as she was half-dragged into the main room with the rest of the mobsters. She may have evaded death for one moment, but much greater trouble loomed. Her mind raced with possibilities, tragedies, and fears, but she shoved the distractions down and focused on one thing – *getting caught was always a part of the plan.*

She put on a pouty face, like a child caught with her hands in a bag of candy before lunch. Inside, she ran through the scenarios she had prepared for. Leonardo Lucianni's own brother, Tony Lucianni, with a henchman on one side, faced down three other mobsters. Those would be representatives of the upstart family, the Callahans. They were making trouble for the Lucianni's but had too much clout in this part of the city to be ignored.

They were all gathered in the center of a large warehouse. High stacks of crates of all sizes formed a shadowy cityscape. The catwalks above were empty and un-patrolled, as was custom for these sorts of meetings. There was a strange honor code among the highest peaks of the bottom of the scuzz barrel. Liars and thieves insisted upon respect and reputation. It was the kind of dissonance that ruled the desperate corners of the lower world. Tonight, that conflict would be her ally.

Her "escort" shoved her to the center of the ring of gangsters and took his place on the flank of the Lucianni boss.

"Hey, watch your hands, all right?" She waved the brute's hands off and smoothed out her long skirt and dingy blouse.

"What kind of trick is this, huh, Tony? You lose one of your secretaries again?" One of the Callahans rubbed his narrow chin with a knotty hand. He looked her up and down as if she were a slab of pork hung in one of their packing freezers.

Tony shook his head. "Not one of mine." He pointed a finger at the Callahan fellow. "And I don't appreciate the insinuation."

The other man closed his mouth, but his brow knitted together as he tried to figure her out.

She had pieced together psychological profiles of the major players in the underworld. Tony Lucianni was a smart man, but quiet, and never acted rashly. Freddy Callahan had a reputation for a quick temper and was exceedingly vindictive. She kept quiet. Let them come to their conclusions. Glancing at the catwalks above, she saw a shadow shift. She smiled inside, as one more piece fell into place.

"We got ourselves a police informant then." Freddy nodded, sure in his conclusion. "Who are you working for? Come on, out with it girl."

"Hey, I gotta make a living somehow." The years surviving in the dirtiest parts of town had washed all traces of sophistication out of her like bleach down a sewer grate. "It wasn't like I had a choice, all right?"

From behind her, the other Lucianni meat mountain placed a heavy hand on her shoulder. She jumped, not feigning nervousness, and turned to see Tony smiling thinly.

"Please, continue." Tony gestured with a hand, all genteel and polite, the serpent tongue hidden.

"Okay, okay!" She shrugged off the large man's hand and hunched her shoulders. "I've been talking with some guy with the government, a Mr. Bradley. He wanted information about some kind of dark angel wings. Look, maybe I could work for you, too, you know? Tell him whatever you want me say?" She looked back and forth between both sides.

"Howard Bradley?" Freddy Callahan stepped back and looked at Tony. "Bradley's your man. How does he know about the Black Wing Angel? What kind of job you trying to pull, huh Tony?" Callahan looked around at everyone present, nodding and coming to conclusions.

She schooled her face to confusion. "What? I don't understand." She kept a sly eye on the Lucianni side. Tony's eyes were narrowed, and she could see the gears turning behind them.

"You've told me plenty enough." Freddy jabbed a finger at Tony. "You're already planning to cross us off, Tony? You getting your boy in the feds in on this? Gonna let them sweep in and clean us up, then move into our turf after?" He shook his head. "Deal's off, Tony. You can tell that to Leonardo Lucianni, himself."

"Shut your mouth, Freddy." Tony spoke. "We never told Mr. Bradley about Black Wing Angel. You think we didn't see what you've been doing the last few months? The side deals, the double-crosses? The Callahans have been playing my brother for a fool. Do you want me to tell *that* to Leonardo Lucianni himself?"

The only thing worse than finding a worm in your apple was finding half a worm. She and Mr. Bradley had spent years laying down tripwires and seeding information between the competing families, allowing their natural distrust to fester. It was boiling beneath the surface, and the lid was just about to pop.

"You're coming with me, missy." Freddy Callahan cocked his head at one of his goons, who reached out to grab her arm. Right before he did so, she jerked her head and body and stumbled, coughing. She slapped a hand to her neck. Red seeped from her fingers, and she fell to the floor. The packet of fake blood spilled its contents over her dirt-stained blouse.

Both the Luciannis and the Callahans shouted, drawing their weapons, some pointing them at each other and others aiming up at the catwalks.

She and Mr. Bradley had spread so much confusion and distrust among these two groups that both families had broken custom and posted guards on the railings above. Everybody fired on everybody. Her cheek pressed against the cold concrete floor as an infernal shower of sparks rained from above. It was a volcanic celebration of light and fury. Bodies hit the floor surrounded by clattering brass casings just ejected from the weapons that dropped from their grasping hands. Hot metal landed on her upraised cheek, but she refused to acknowledge the pain. Instead, she looked into the eyes of mobster after mobster as they fell around her, catching each blank and empty stare.

The quiet of the grave descended upon the warehouse. She waited for three minutes, ticking off the seconds in her head. Nobody stirred.

Finally, she breathed deeply and stood up. It had worked. One of the most tense and critical meetings of the two most powerful crime families in the city had ended with everyone dead. The rippling consequences would envelop the entire underworld, and the remaining cockroaches would stumble into all the other pit traps she and Mr. Bradley had laid for them.

There was one last task: recover the Black Wing Angel. If it was a drug, Freddy Callahan wouldn't have it on him. It would be stashed nearby, ready to be given to the Luciannis as a token.

She spotted movement coming from a darkened warehouse office thirty feet away. After snatching her handbag and the Colt from the Lucianni who had found her in the atrium, she crept to the open doorway. She chambered a round and cocked the hammer, standing flush against the outer door frame. She would have to be fast and take out any survivors. If word got out this had all been a setup, her work would be ruined.

Spinning into the room with the gun raised, she barely stopped herself from blowing a hole in the chest of a young woman tied to a broken office chair. Veronica gasped and held the wall for support, feeling lightheaded as a flood of tension rushed out of her body. Fingers finding a switch, she turned on the light.

The young woman was maybe eighteen or nineteen years old, barely more than a girl. She had a rag stuffed in her mouth and secured around her head, and her wrists and ankles were bound with twine. She shook the chair with a vigor that belied her small frame. Her big dark eyes were framed by raven locks hanging long and straight down the sides of her pale face like the black wings of an angel.

"It's okay, honey," Veronica said, "you're safe now."

The young beauty didn't have the look of a mule—not nearly enough bruises. Was she the Black Wing Angel herself? It was all so familiar – her son's classmate in the van, the girl in her own class along with her older sister – trafficking in young women was the hot new drug trade of the criminal underground. Veronica pulled the rags free of her mouth and retrieved a pocketknife out of her handbag. She repeated her reassurances, but the girl remained silent. She had a shadowed look to her eyes and only flinched as Veronica sawed through her wrist bonds. What was so important about this one girl?

A silencer coughed in the outer warehouse, and Veronica felt a searing fire in her middle. She fell to a knee inside the office, twisting around to see Freddy Callahan just outside with his eyes blazing with hate, his tattered chest oozing blood. He collapsed to the dust, dropping his pistol from his outstretched hand. "Double crossing ..." The rest of his words dribbled away into a death rattle.

The girl screamed.

Veronica collapsed like a marionette with its strings cut, her pocketknife clattering to the floor. A rose blossomed on the white linen of Veronica's blouse, and her lifeblood pooled on the floor, reflecting the flickering fluorescent lights above.

The young woman fell out of the office chair and grabbed the knife, cutting through the rest of the twine with a maddened frenzy.

Veronica remembered everything she had done—from blushing brides at her side, to the first rank pinned on her lapel, to the birth of her son. She had sacrificed so much to get to this point so she could slip into the underworld unsuspected. She wouldn't get to see her son graduate, get married, fall in love, or become a father. She wouldn't be there for it, but Cory was safe – he would get to do all those things and more. Now, at the end, she was lying in a pool of her own blood on the dingy floor of an old office. She hadn't even had a good breakfast that morning.

As Veronica Gardner's vision began to slip, the girl clutched her hands to her chest, then her mouth, shouting something Veronica couldn't understand. Was it her first time seeing a gunshot victim? The young lady looked so much like her decades ago. It was close to the reflection in the mirror that she used to see, before the glass became darkened. Before it had shattered.

Those shards of glass rearranged in her mind. Even broken, they could still be shaped. Sometimes, when glass is stained, it creates a beautiful mosaic of light. There was one more thing she could do—one last gift. Was it fate? Was tonight always going to end this way? Perhaps.

With the last bit of her strength, Veronica grabbed the young woman's hands and pulled her close. She placed her palms against the young woman's and spoke.

"Seven-seven-seven Northwest Highlane. Number forty-four. Everything you need. Become Veronica Gardner. Go, and live."

The young woman said something, but Veronica was already slipping away. The last sound that serenaded her into eternity was the soft pattering of feet fleeing into the night.

***

The young woman hugged her knees, sitting on the floor of a small office. There was no name on the outer door, just the number forty-four. She had found keys in the older woman's purse, which she'd snatched before she'd run. Inside the office was a desk, a few battered filing cabinets, a torn leather couch, and a screened-off kitchenette and washroom. Shadows covered everything. She dared not turn on the single lamp perched on the edge of the cheap wooden desk like a dime-store gargoyle.

A garish spear of light pierced the stillness of the office, swept through, and was gone.

The peal of sirens across town warbled again, rising high before descending low. The rulers of the city were in a panic. Only a few hours had passed since she'd fled the warehouse, yet she had felt the tension on the streets as she ran. It was the calm that saturated the sky right before a summer storm—the heavy air just beginning its chaotic rustling of the trees, a distant flash on the darkening boundaries of sight.

Now, the storm was breaking. A chopper thrummed past the building, searchlight passing through the windows, panes rattling in their casements. The whispers were hitting the ears that mattered. They would speak of death, of thrones toppled, of the order of the underworld upended. All because of Veronica Gardner.

The young woman held a battered piece of glossy paper up to the light from outside. She had found it in the handbag, stuck under the lining behind an old, outdated ID. A beautiful lady with straight raven hair smiled with a few other people on a boat in a lake. One of them looked young enough to be the woman's son. Faded ink on the back read "Veronica, Cory, Will" along with a date several years ago. Was this Veronica's family? She set the picture down. She wanted to burn it, to remove all traces of anyone who had seen her tied up, gagged, and turned into a product for sale.

"Become Veronica Gardner." Those were among the last words the stranger, her savior, had said to her. How was that possible? Even ignoring the practical, how could she possibly take on another person? She had her own history, her own problems. She knew nothing of whatever baggage Veronica brought with her. No, she needed to do what she always did—take whatever she needed, keep her head down, and look out for herself as best she could. Veronica had freed her from the Callahans tonight, but that was as far as it could go.

Heavy footfalls thumped on the rancid carpet in the outside hallway. She held her breath, keeping in the shadows beneath another search beam. Were the authorities going building to building, floor by floor? How could she hide, then? What was so important about that meeting in the warehouse?

The steps stopped in front of the office door. She saw the shadows of a pair of feet through the crack at the bottom of the warped wood. She strained to listen, but the pulsing blood coursing through her head drowned out other sounds. There was heavy thud, like a bag hitting the floor, and the steps receded. A shadow under the door remained.

A shrill ring shattered the silence, and a telephone on the desk bounced and clattered. Who on earth could be calling at this time of night? It had to be connected to the incident at the warehouse. The line of shadow under the door grew to her eyes, encompassing the whole office. What was in that bag, and who was calling Veronica Gardner moments after its delivery?

She tried to shut it all out of her mind, but the ringing didn't abate. Finally, if just to end it all, she snatched up the heavy handset and pressed it to her ear.

"Yes?" Her voice cracked, and she swallowed.

"Fine work tonight." A deep voice, male, older but clear. Hints of authority. Exactly the sort she had spent the last several years learning to fear.

"Thank you." She kept her voice small. The less she spoke, the less this man could spot her as an imposter. If this was the Mr. Bradley she had heard Veronica and the others speak of, every word could be dangerous.

"The underworld is in a feeding frenzy. What you did will ripple out and bring down their entire criminal empire. Generations ahead will have you to thank."

Not me. Her. Who had Veronica been, really?

"This is where we go our separate ways," he said. "Like we discussed, all contact from my office will cease. Financial support will end." Mr. Bradley paused. "Well, except for one last gift. I managed to tuck away a lump sum from my budget to see you off."

Was that what was in the bag? She peered at the shadow on the floor in the hallway. "Hold on a moment." She set the phone on the desk and creaked open the outside door. A large canvas duffle bag had been dropped there. She retrieved it and unzipped it, gasping as she shouldered the phone to her ear.

Mr. Bradley cleared his throat. "You really did go above and beyond."

Bundled stacks of bills filled up the bag, and a manila envelope rested atop the pile. There had to be tens of thousands of dollars in there. Panic climbed up her throat. What had she stumbled into?

"One hundred thousand dollars in unmarked, untraceable bills. In the envelope, you'll find new credentials for Veronica. I have to congratulate you. Despite diving into the muck of the streets, you still kept your nose clean. I didn't have to sanitize your ID—Veronica Gardner is already clear."

Her mind spun as the implications began to settle in. Money, a new life, a fresh start. Was it possible? No way. Things like this didn't happen to her.

"How?" She gripped the phone tight. There had to be a loophole, a trap.

The older man chuckled on the phone. "Because I can. More than that, I want to. Not everyone has to be so covered in grime that the shine is forever lost. You can burn brightly again, Veronica." He paused. "Just not here. You'll need to leave town. Go to the countryside, maybe a small town somewhere in the Midwest. You cut the past before. Now, you'll need to do it again—but this time in victory."

"Okay." One-word replies. She was beginning to trust this man, and that terrified her more than anything else that had happened that night.

"This is the last time you'll hear from me. Know that I won't ever forget what you did, for everyone."

What she *did. Not me.*

"Before I hang up, I have one question. The local uniforms at the crime scene reported a Jane Doe. Straight black hair, young. Who was she?"

"She was..." She faltered. Who was she? A nobody? A victim? A Black Wing Angel? "She saved my life, but I never caught her name."

"Hmm. Interesting." She could hear a small smile in his voice. "Go and live, Veronica." The line clicked, silent.

She sank into the couch, letting the phone call tumble around in her mind. Go and live. Veronica had said the exact same words. Where? She was now anonymous. She couldn't return to her wealthy parents—the ones who had used her as a political pawn, feigning horror and grief on the evening news, vowing to shake the world apart to find her, all the while gaining fame and power from her kidnapping. Even the foreign diplomat who had bought her from traffickers had treated her with more care, though his attentions came with another kind of abuse. Then there were the Callahans, who were ready to sell her to gain advantage. They had said she was going back to her family, but it was all a lie. More likely, her abduction had been arranged from the start. She had no home to which she could return.

Within the black lake of despair that was her soul, a little spark was slowly flickering. It was something she hadn't felt since she was a very small child—hope. She had seen the compassion in Veronica's eyes. She had heard the submerged warmth in Mr. Bradley's voice. Somebody, somewhere, genuinely cared about her.

She picked up the picture where she had dropped it on the floor and smoothed out the wrinkles and folds. The other woman smiled at her, and she smiled back. Maybe one day she could track down the people in the photo and let them know what Veronica had done for her. She pressed the photo to her chest. She was going to keep this and keep it close—in remembrance of the woman who died so she could live.

She walked to the window and looked out upon the city. The frenzy of sirens was dying down, and she didn't flinch when a bright beam passed over her as a chopper arced by. Her past had been washed away, wiped clean by the sacrifice of a stranger. She no longer had reason to fear the light. The gray glow of predawn lit the sky beyond the city. There was a whole world out there.

She was Veronica Gardner, and for the first time in her life, she could become anything she wanted.

AUTHOR BIOS/LINKS

Shannon D. Pearson is a former band nerd and holds degrees in American Sign Language and accounting. She loves her role as a wife and homeschooling mother of a growing family. Pen and paper are her tools. After all, stories can be handwritten while cradling a baby.

She and her family live in the same city where she grew up in Oklahoma. She's attended the same church since in her mother's womb, a legacy her children are continuing.

Her alter ego, "paperclip girl," fights chaos with organization, and you shouldn't be surprised to see Shannon wearing paperclips.

Shannon can be found at https://www.facebook.com/Shannon-D-Pearson-writes-13892765537858950/

David L. Thornburg is the author of the Oak Valley Secrets series, which uses his home state of Oklahoma for colorful characters, vivid settings, and bizarre history.

David can often be found hanging out with his first reader and wife Kelly. He has a dog the size of a small horse and likes Star Trek more than he should. In their day jobs, David and Kelly work with Special Needs students at a public school.

He can be reached at https://www.facebook.com/davidlthornburgauthor

Sign up at his website http://davidlthornburg.wix.com/mysite and receive a free short story, *Sooner Wed: Oak Valley Secrets 1.5.*

Kristi Woods is an award-winning storyteller, weaving fiction and nonfiction writings with strong threads of faith. But mostly she's a Jesus girl who, along with her family, survived a nomadic, military lifestyle. She and her family have set roots in Oklahoma, where she keeps a close watch for tornadoes and good chocolate. Join her email list at *KristiWoods.net* for notice of new writings, books, downloadable Bible studies, and free faith encouragement.

Bill Garrison lives in Oklahoma City with his wife four kids and works in the healthcare industry. He is the bestselling author of the Christian time-travel mystery, *THE DAY SHE DIED.*

Katherine Webster is a writer, teacher, and counselor specialized in the field of child and adolescent development. Katherine Webster wrote her first article in sixth grade for the school newspaper. Her articles on child development and parenting have been published in the *Daily Oklahoman*. During her educational career, she has witnessed great changes in students and families.

She is finally getting to write her own stories and poetry. She is a member of the Oklahoma writers club and Creatives Quills. Katherine lives in Edmond, Oklahoma, with her husband and her dog Macie. While not writing, she is a monthly chairperson for a self-help group, plays pickleball, and attends yoga class.

Chris Tarpley once moonlighted in the IT industry, but his heart has always been devoted to storytelling. He lives in rural Oklahoma with his wife and son, two dogs, a cat, and the occasional field mouse that evades the traps. Chris is a contributing author of *The Legacy Letters*, *Cracked Ice*, *By This Sign*, and *Secrets, Spies and Allies*. He is currently working on *City of Ruins*, book one of the Virid Flame series of fantasy novels. Follow him at www.christarpleybooks.com[1]

---

1. http://www.christarpleybooks.com

Additional Collections
by OCFW Writers
https://www.okchristianfictionwriters.com
Heart of Christmas

When Eleanor Clark arrives home for the holidays, the last thing she expects is to run into her high school crush Tad Varner—in her mother's living room. The first Christmas without her brother will be heartbreaking enough—now she has to face the one man she's never been able to put behind her?

Christmas is supposed to be a time for family, gifts, and faith. The Clarks have been Tad's only real family, but he isn't sure he buys into their faith anymore, not after losing his best friend—Eleanor's twin brother. When sparks fly between him and Ellie, will they ignite the faith he left behind or burn them both?

by Bill Garrison, Robin Patchen, Sharon Srock, Terri Denise Weldon, and Lacy Williams

The Legacy Letters

Seven pink envelopes, addressed in Wanda Taylor's spiky handwriting, represented her legacy to seven people she held dear. Legacy letters—that's what they were. A last gift, though some might call it interference. People often sought her advice and her God-given gift of discernment. But not these seven, and her heart ached for them. They were good people who loved God and their families, but she saw patterns in their lives that could harm them in the future if left unchecked. Monica was the lynchpin of the entire project. The mantle of the matriarch fit her, and everyone in the family recognized it. But she needed to learn how to let go before she could take charge. Monica would receive the first letter, one month after Wanda's death. The others—to friends, siblings, children, and grandchildren—would receive their letters in the six months following. Wanda sealed the last letter and whispered a prayer. "Lord, use my words a final time to do Your work in the lives of those I leave behind."

by Darlene Franklin, Jessica Ferguson, Ruth Collins, Martha Fouts, J.J. Johnson, Alanna Radle Rodriguez, and Chris Tarpley

Cracked Ice

One December night, an ice storm blows through Oklahoma City, leaving thousands without power. Meet the residents of Primrose Apartments. Young, old, alone, in love, prey, and predator. What happens when the lights go out?

by Darlene Franklin, Toni Chism, Bill Garrison, Kat Lewis, Sue Merriam, Shannon D. Pearson, and Chris Tarpley

18 Redbud Lane

Six generations build a legacy of faith on the Oklahoma prairie.

by Vickie McDonough, Kathryn Spurgeon, Shannon D. Pearson, Kat Lewis, Alanna Radle Rodriguez, and T. J. Radle

By This Sign

This is the sign of life and death. Beginning and the end. Alpha and omega. Now—it's the only way you will ever get home again. Let the adventure begin.

by Shannon D. Pearson, Terri Walters, Darlene Franklin, Bill Garrison, T. J. Radle, B. M. Stevenson, Robert Andrew Stevenson, Kat Lewis, and Chris Tarpley

Secrets, Spies, and Allies

The Grand Game by B.M. Stevenson

The love of her life has gone missing, and double agent Rose Travers must employ all her skills in espionage to find him. But D-Day is fast approaching, demanding all her attention. Will this war make her choose between the good of one and the good of many?

The End is Not the End by Robert Andrew Stevenson

Brothers Eugene and Henry have been thick as thieves since childhood. But growing up means facing new challenges around every corner, including the cold, dark days of the besiegement of Bastogne. This war is going to change them both. Will it be for the better?

The Golden Lions by Shannon D. Pearson

Sam's secret managed to survive basic training. When their regiment is captured and they are shipped off to German POW camps, Byron learns the truth about his best friend and training partner. If the enemy finds out, it could mean the end of Sam's life.

Eraser by Chris Tarpley

Elias lost his wife and child back home, yet he sees them with his waking eyes. Plagued by grief, he must maintain his sanity for one final mission—to infiltrate Wewelsberg, the infamous dark castle of the Nazi SS. Will Elias be able to discern reality from phantasm long enough to save the living from the dead?